"I'm Pregnant. Over Two Months Along, And You're The Father."

Pregnant?

Shock hit him square in the solar plexus. Followed by disbelief. Then jaded acceptance of her betrayal. Just when he'd thought he couldn't be any more disillusioned by how easily people could deceive others. A bitter laugh rolled around in his gut and burned a bilious path up his throat.

She crossed her arms under her breasts defensively. "If this is some kind of payback for my laughter earlier, I don't appreciate it. I don't find this in the least amusing."

"Believe me, neither do I."

Her mouth went tight, her anger palpable. "This isn't going to make much of a story to tell our child some day."

"*Our* child? I think not."

Dear Reader,

Welcome to the final book in my Rich, Rugged & Royal series! In *The Maverick Prince,* we were introduced to Antonio, the shipping magnate and youngest of the Medina men. In *His Thirty-Day Fiancée,* we saw the second Medina son, Duarte, meet his match. And now it's time to learn more about the oldest son, Carlos, dedicated doctor and heir to a defunct kingdom.

During the violent coup to overthrow the Medina monarchy, Carlos sustained injuries that left him with a permanent limp and no hope of ever having a family of his own. Or so he thinks! His preconceptions are blown out of the water when his long-time friend and one-time lover surprises him with the news that she is carrying his child, his heir, their future.

I hope you enjoy the last installment to my Medina trilogy. As always, I enjoy hearing from readers and can be reached through my website, www.catherinemann.com, or at my mailing address, P.O. Box 6065, Navarre, FL 32566.

Happy Reading!

Catherine Mann

CATHERINE MANN

HIS HEIR, HER HONOR

Silhouette® Desire

Published by Silhouette Books
America's Publisher of Contemporary Romance

To my children, my own little princes and princesses,
even though they're not so little anymore.
Brice, Haley, Robbie and Maggie—I love you!

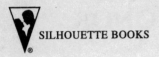

SILHOUETTE BOOKS

ISBN-13: 978-0-373-73084-1

Recycling programs
for this product may
not exist in your area.

HIS HEIR, HER HONOR

Copyright © 2011 by Catherine Mann

Visit Silhouette Books at www.eHarlequin.com

Printed in U.S.A.

Books by Catherine Mann

Silhouette Desire

Baby, I'm Yours #1721
Under the Millionaire's Influence #1787
The Executive's Surprise Baby #1837
†*Rich Man's Fake Fiancée* #1878
†*His Expectant Ex* #1895
Propositioned Into a Foreign Affair #1941
†*Millionaire in Command* #1969
Bossman's Baby Scandal #1988
†*The Tycoon Takes a Wife* #2013
Winning It All #2031
  "Pregnant with the Playboy's Baby"
The Maverick Prince #2047
His Thirty-Day Fiancée 2061
His Heir, Her Honor 2071

†The Landis Brothers
*Rich, Rugged & Royal

CATHERINE MANN

USA TODAY bestselling author Catherine Mann is living out her own fairy-tale ending on a sunny Florida beach with her Prince Charming husband and their four children. With more than thirty-five books in print in more than twenty countries, she has also celebrated wins for both a RITA® Award and a Booksellers' Best Award. Catherine enjoys chatting with readers online—thanks to the wonders of the wireless internet that allows her to network with her laptop by the water! To learn more about her work, visit her website, www.catherinemann.com, or reach her by snail mail at P.O. Box 6065, Navarre, FL 32566.

Dear Reader,

Yes, it's true. We're changing our name! After more than twenty-five years of being part of Harlequin Enterprises, Silhouette Books will officially seal the merger by taking the company's name.

So if you notice a few changes on the covers starting April 2011—Silhouette Special Edition becoming Harlequin Special Edition, Silhouette Desire becoming Harlequin Desire, and Silhouette Romantic Suspense becoming Harlequin Romantic Suspense—don't be concerned.

We'll continue to have the same fantastic authors, wonderful stories, eye-catching covers and emotional, compelling reads. We're just going to be moving under the overall company name, which will make us even easier for you to see in the stores, on the internet and wherever you usually find us!

So look for the new logo, but remember, beneath the image will be the same promise of romantic stories of love, passion, adventure, family and a whole lot more. Just the way you like them!

Sincerely,

The Editors at Harlequin Books

One

"Cover the family jewels, gentlemen," Lilah Anderson called into the men's locker room at St. Mary's Hospital. "Female coming through."

High heels clicking on tile, Lilah charged past a male nurse yanking on scrubs and an anesthesiologist wrestling with a too-small towel, barely registering the flash of male flank here, masculine chest there. Smothered coughs and chuckles echoed around her in the steamy tiled area, but she remained undeterred.

Completely focused on locating *him*.

No one dared stop her on her way past benches and lockers. As chief administrator of Tacoma's leading surgical facility, she could have any of them fired faster than someone could say "Who dropped the soap?"

Her only problem? A particularly stubborn employee who seemed determined to avoid her every attempt to speak with him over the past couple of weeks. Therefore, she'd chosen the one place she could be certain of having Dr. Carlos Medina's complete attention—a public shower.

The stall tactics would end here and now. And speaking of stalls...

Lilah stepped deeper into the swell of steam puffing around a cream-colored plastic curtain. His secretary, Wanda, had warned that he couldn't be reached since he was washing up after a lengthy surgery. He would be exhausted and cranky.

Not deterred in the least, Lilah saw this as the perfect opportunity she'd been seeking to corner him. She'd grown up with two brothers, and she would have been left out of everything if she didn't occasionally invade their male inner sanctums. She eyed the line of showers.

Three of the five were in use. The first sported a shadowy, short and round male figure. Not Carlos.

From the second, a balding head peeked around the industrial curtain with shocked green eyes. Also not her surgeon in question.

She nodded to the head of pediatrics. "Good afternoon, Jim."

Jim ducked back into his stall, which left her to focus on the third tiled cubicle. She marched forward, heels tapping almost as fast as her heart.

Stopping, she planted her feet and checked first. Through the plastic folds, she studied the lean outline standing under the spray, scrubbing his hands over his head. Without even pulling aside the curtain, she knew that body well, intimately so.

She'd found him, Carlos Medina—doctor, lover and,

as if the guy didn't already have enough going for him, also the eldest son of a former European monarch. His princely pedigree, however, didn't impress her. Long before she knew about his royal roots, she'd been drawn to his brilliance, his compassion for his patients….

And a backside that looked damn fine in scrubs. Or wearing nothing at all. Definitely not what she needed to think about right now.

Lilah gathered her nerve as firmly as she clenched the curtain and swept it aside, metal rings *clink, clink, clinking* along the rod.

A wall of steam rolled out, momentarily clouding her vision until the mist dispersed and exposed an eyeful of mouthwateringly magnificent *man*. Water sluiced down Carlos's naked body turned sideways, revealing long lean muscles flexing and bunching. And heaven help her, she had a perfect view of the curve of his taut butt.

Beads of moisture clung to his bronzed skin, arms and legs sprinkled with dark hair. No tan lines marked him since he spent most of his time indoors either in surgery or asleep. But his natural olive coloring gave him an allover tanned look, as if he'd bared himself unabashedly to the sun.

As he turned his head toward her in a slow, deliberate move, not even a whisper of surprise showed on Carlos's face. His eyes shone nearly black…heavy lidded…darkly enigmatic. She couldn't suppress a shiver of desire as his intense gaze held hers. Her stomach knotted with a traitorous ache that could only serve to distract her from her mission today.

He raised one thick eyebrow, slashing upward into his forehead. "Yes?"

His subtle Spanish accent saturated the lone syllable like the steam in the air, so hot she felt the urge to ditch the jacket on her power suit.

In the next stall, water shut off in a hurry as the head of pediatrics made a hasty departure from the locker room. Others lingered, backs studiously turned as they retrieved clothing.

Lilah tugged her jacket more firmly in place. "I need to talk to you."

"A telephone conversation would have saved my coworkers some embarrassment." He spoke softly as always, never raising his voice as if he knew innately that people would hang on his every word.

"What I have to say isn't for an impersonal call." And wasn't that the understatement of the year? What she needed to tell him also wasn't for the curious ears behind her, but she would have Carlos alone soon.

All alone?

Static-like awareness popped along her nerves until the hair on her arms rose. Was that an answering spark lighting his dark eyes? Then he blinked away any hint of emotion.

"It does not get much more personal than this, boss lady." He turned off the shower. "Could you pass me that towel?"

She snagged the white cotton draped on a hook. The hospital name and logo were stamped along the bottom. She pitched the towel to him rather than risk an accidental touch. As he looped it around his waist, she couldn't resist staring for a stolen second.

Water soaked his hair even blacker, shiny and swept back from his face. Every hard and hunky angle of his aristocratic cheekbones and nose was revealed. Dark brows slashed over brown eyes that rarely carried humor, but turned lava lush when he made love to her.

Pivoting, his back to her for the first time, he snagged his shampoo. Her eyes quickly left his slim hips and taut butt, drawn more to the scars along his lower back. In the four years she'd known him, he'd chalked up his permanent limp to a teenage riding accident. The one time she'd pressed him, the first time she'd seen those scars, he'd brushed aside further questions with distracting kisses along her bare skin.

While she was a lawyer and not a doctor, her tenure working at the hospital—and flat-out common sense—clued her in that he'd suffered a major physical trauma.

Toiletries bag tucked under his arm, he leaned toward her. His shoulders, then his eyes, drew her in until the rest of the space faded away. She swallowed hard.

He stared back, unblinking, unflinching. "Let's make this quick."

"Your charm never ceases to impress me."

"If you're looking for charm, you hired the wrong man four years ago." He'd been thirty-six then to her thirty-one, a lifetime ago. "I've spent most of the day repairing the spine of a seven-year-old Afghani girl injured by a roadside bomb. I'm beat."

Unwanted sympathy whispered through her. Of course he was exhausted from the drawn-out, tragic surgery. Even when he caved to his pride and used a chair during extended operations, the toll it took on him was always evident. But she couldn't afford to weaken now.

They'd been friends for years only to have him turn into a cold jackass because of an impulsive one-night

. stand together after a Christmas fundraiser. It wasn't like she'd dropped a wedding planner in his lap five seconds after the third orgasm waned.

Yep, *three*. Her toes curled inside her pumps at just the memory of each shimmering release.

The sex had been amazing. Beyond amazing actually, and after that impulsive hookup, she'd envisioned them transitioning into a relationship of friends with kick-ass benefits. A nerve-tingling, *safe* option. But he'd pulled away as fast as he'd pulled on his pants the next morning. He was cold, withdrawn and *painfully* polite.

But she wasn't backing down. "I don't have the time for niceties. I'm just here to say my piece. So grab some clothes and let's talk."

He ducked his head until his voice heated her ear. "You're not the type to create a scene. Let's set up a time to talk when you're calmer. This is already awkward enough."

Her nose twitched at his fresh-washed scent. Yes, she'd chosen an unconventional route for her confrontation, but Carlos Medina's tenacious—stubborn—reputation was legendary. She felt confident the hospital board would cut her a little slack for her scene. And if they didn't? Then so be it. Sometimes a woman had to make a stand.

This was her time. She couldn't afford to wait much longer.

"I'm not setting up an appointment. I'm not delaying this conversation." She lowered her voice, although from the sound of retreating footsteps behind her there must not be many people left. "We talk. Today. The only matter up for discussion is whether we chat right here in front of everyone or if we speak in an office. And believe me, if we stay here, it's going to get a lot more awkward very quickly."

Carlos cocked an eyebrow.

From behind her, a cleared throat echoed, or a stifled laugh perhaps. She looked up at Carlos, suddenly painfully aware of just how close they stood to each other with nothing but a towel covering his oh-so-generous family jewels.

Whispering, she struggled not to back away—or move closer still. Carlos had ignored her for nearly three months, hurtful and flat-out insulting given their friendship. Or rather, their *prior* friendship.

One way or another, she would get a reaction from him. "It's not like I haven't seen you before. In fact, I recall in great—"

"Enough," he silenced her with a word.

"The almighty Medina prince has spoken," she mocked, backing a step to snag surgical scrubs from the top of a stack. "Get dressed. I'll wait."

She thrust the folded green set his way and turned away. A trio of half-dressed men faced her, their jaws slack and eyes wide. The magnitude of the scene she'd caused hit her full on for the first time. She resisted the urge to squirm.

This was too important to show any vulnerability. She just hoped she could maintain enough distance to get through the conversation during their first time alone together in so long. She pressed her fingers to her lips, still unable to forget the rush of passion from their first impetuous kiss, a clench that had led to so much more with lasting consequences.

Once Carlos put on his clothes and they moved to another room, he would learn the truth she'd only just begun to accept herself. A truth she could no longer avoid.

Dr. Carlos Medina was a little over six months away from becoming a princely papa.

Carlos Medina was about six seconds away from losing his temper, something he never, never allowed to happen.

Of course, *he* was the person who needed chewing out for foolishly allowing himself to sleep with Lilah nearly three months ago. He'd wrecked a top-notch working relationship.

Sidestepping a janitor slopping an ammonia-saturated mop over the floor, Carlos followed her down the otherwise empty hospital walkway, wearing fresh surgical scrubs, tennis shoes and ten tons of frustration. Fluorescent lights overhead lined the path down the corridor. Windows flanked either side. Murky late day sun fought to pierce the dreary drizzle outdoors. But his focus was locked in on the woman two steps ahead of him on the way to his office.

His office. Not hers. His territory.

She may have tipped the controls in her favor with the shower confrontation, but he wasn't giving ground again. His office would also provide guaranteed privacy. Once his Medina name had been exposed, the hospital had been flooded with paparazzi. He'd feared he might have to resign his position in order to ensure the safety of his patients.

But he'd underestimated Lilah.

She'd slapped restraining orders and injunctions on the press in a flash. She'd increased security at the hospital. And she'd moved his office to the farthest corner of the building. Overzealous paparazzi would have to run a gauntlet of two layers of security and a half-dozen heavily populated nurses' stations before reaching his newly relocated inner sanctum. No one in the press had succeeded to date.

Yes, he'd underestimated her then, something he wouldn't do now. He needed every edge he could muster around this woman when all he could think about was her bold entrance into his shower, her gaze raking over his body as if she wouldn't mind a touch. A taste. Maybe even a bite. Damn, but he hadn't expected to see her again without the defense of even a pair of boxers.

The understated twitch of her hips encased in a black power suit held his gaze far longer than any simple passing interest. His eyes glided up the rigid brace of her spine to the vulnerable curve of her neck, exposed with her auburn hair swept into a tight twist. One stubborn curl escaped to caress her ear the way he burned to do even now when he was angry as hell with her.

He'd wanted her for years, but knew she was the one woman he had to keep his hands well off. She was too insightful, too good of a friend and one who mirrored his workaholic ways. Anything more than a professional friendship would be disastrous. For a man who'd had precious few friends in his life, he'd valued the unexpected camaraderie he'd found with Lilah.

Clearing the hall and entering his reception area, he tore his eyes away from the enticing curve of her butt and nodded to his secretary, an efficient woman with photos of her twelve grandchildren neatly lined up on her desk. "Hold my calls, Wanda, unless it's about the Afghani girl in recovery."

His back twinged with a reminder of just how long

he'd spent cleaning up bone fragments along the child's spine, of working to relieve pressure, doing all he could to ensure she had as much use of her arms as possible even though she would almost certainly never walk again. Entering his office, he braced a hand on the door frame, then the sofa, using walls and furniture to steady himself at the end of a long day. His uneven gait contrasted with the efficient click of Lilah's killer red heels.

Skimming her fingers along a row of leather-bound medical journals, she stopped in front of a framed oil painting by Joaquín Sorolla y Bastida, a gift from his middle brother, Duarte. The canvas came from Bastida's *Sad Inheritance* preparatory pieces, a painting of crippled children bathing in healing waters.

No matter how much distance Carlos put between himself and his homeland, influences from his heritage called to him. He couldn't escape the reality of being the oldest son of deposed King Enrique Medina from San Rinaldo, a small island country off the coast of Spain. He couldn't ignore or forget how his father had fled with his family, relocating to live anonymously off the coast of Florida for decades.

Only recently had the press picked up the Medina trail. Carlos and his two brothers, all now adults, lived in different locations across the United States. Until four months ago, they'd even managed to fly under the radar with assumed names.

For most of his adult life he'd been known as Carlos Santiago. Yet in the stroke of a media pen's exposé, it became impossible for people to think of him as anything other than Carlos Medina, heir to a defunct monarchy.

Lilah was the one person who hadn't treated him differently after the news had broken about his Medina heritage. She hadn't been impressed or even angry over his years of deception. She understood his reasons for keeping his identity hidden.

The only question she'd asked after the story broke? As the hospital's administrator, she'd requested verification that all his medical credentials were valid and in order, given his assumed name.

She was a logical woman to the end.

So what the hell made a sensible person like Lilah decide to waltz into the men's locker room and confront him in the shower? A confrontation that still had him imagining scenarios where he pulled her under the spray with him to peel off every stitch of her clothing until she was as naked and hungry as him.

He closed the door to his office, sealing them inside the sparse space. He kept his world streamlined, only bare essential leather furniture, the painting from his brother and his books.

Leaning back against the wall to take pressure off his aching spine, he faced Lilah for the first time since she'd stared him down through a thin veil of mist. Her back was still straight but her face was pale. Very pale.

Worry whispered over him as his doctor senses blared an alert. She was obviously under great stress. Only extreme measures would have driven her to act so rashly. Normally, she calmly presented her case and made her move, with a legal eagle precision that served to make her a top-notch lawyer with a fast-track start to a brilliant career. He should have realized that. He mentally kicked himself for assuming her confrontation had something to do with their encounter two and a half months ago.

Carlos studied her green eyes, noting the dark circles beneath. "Is it bad news about funding for the new rehab wing?"

"This isn't about work…." She hesitated, chewing the red lipstick from her kissably full mouth.

Concern scratched deeper. He pushed away from the door toward her, drawn by threads of their old friendship and the scent of her perfume. If he whispered in her ear again as he had earlier, he would smell a hint of her body wash along her neck. Not a heavy perfume by any means given the hospital's fairly strict rules about scented lotions, soaps and colognes. Just enough pure Lilah to send his heart pumping faster.

Her eyes tracked him and each uneven step, his limp aggravated by the hours he'd spent operating today. Long ago, he'd gotten over any self-consciousness. Life held much more important issues and concerns than whether people noticed the impairment or pitied him. He knew he was damn lucky to be walking at all.

He closed the space between them. "Then what's so important that you felt the need to cause a scene big enough to feed hospital cafeteria gossip for at least a month?"

"It's about what happened after the Christmas fundraiser."

He stopped short. With a few simple words, she filled the room with memories of the night they'd stumbled back here, into his office, then finished the night at his house because it was closer than her condo. The memories were too vivid, so close on the heels of her bold move striding into the shower. Good thing she'd passed him the towel so fast because he'd been damn close to presenting her with an unmistakable visual on how much she still moved him. Turning his back to her under the pretense of gathering his soap had offered him a few seconds to scavenge control of his careening libido.

He'd been reckless enough to cave into the temptation to sleep with her once before. Every day since then, he'd been tormented by reliving that night and knowing just how easy it would be to succumb to temptation again. Still feeling the near-tangible caress of her eyes on him from earlier, he tried to remember all the reasons he should keep his hands off her.

Somehow his finger landed on the lone curl teasing around the shell-like curve of her ear. The softness of her skin, the silky texture of her hair wrapping around his touch as if drawing him closer, each nuance of Lilah tapped aside the paper-thin remains of his restraint.

Awareness glinted in her jewel tone eyes a second before he cupped the back of her neck and stepped toward her, until God help him, every curve of her body pressed to him in a perfect fit. The give of her breasts, the cradle of her hips, the familiar feel of her broadsided his senses with memories of their night together.

"Carlos," she whispered, her palms flat against his chest, pressing, "you're so damn arrogant."

But she swayed into him anyway. His brain shut down a second before he sealed his mouth to hers.

Need knifed through him with surgical precision, sharp and inescapable. She tensed slightly before gripping the front of his scrubs, her fists tight, insistent and more than a little angry as she hauled him closer. The taste of her, the sweep of her tongue meeting his stroke for stroke reminded him of how quickly they could combust. Keeping his distance the past weeks had been necessary and futile all at once.

This was inevitable. Spearing his fingers into her hair, he loosened the tight roll until silken strands cascaded over his skin. How easy it would be to sweep aside her suit and ditch his surgical scrubs. His leather sofa beckoned from across the room.

His desk was closer.

Sweeping his hand along smooth mahogany, he cleared a penholder, calendar and notepad in one efficient swipe that sent the lot clattering to the floor. He angled her back, cupped her bottom, hitched her up onto the edge. He released the top button on her suit jacket, a satiny camisole of some sort gliding over the backs of his knuckles.

Writhing, she moaned encouragement against his mouth and he made quick work of the fastenings, one after the other until he stroked aside the suit coat to reveal her silver, body-hugging shell. He kissed and nipped along her jaw, down her neck, trekking his way to the generous swell of her breasts. His memory hadn't done her justice. As he nuzzled the scented valley, her head lolled back. He tugged her camisole from her skirt and tucked his hand into the waistband, palming the slight curve of her stomach.

Lilah froze in his arms.

The chill radiating off her brought him back to earth like a shower turned icy cold. Months of restraint had gone down the drain in one impulsive moment. He pulled himself from her and leaned against the desk beside her, dragging in air as she yanked her jacket back on with shaky hands, her hair trapped inside.

He needed to fix this mess of his own making. "Lilah, clearly I have made an error in attempting to ignore what happened between us after the Christmas fundraiser. We need to figure out a way to deal with it so we can regain a level working environment."

"Damn straight, it happened." She thrust the buttons through openings with fierce speed, the fabric flower pin on her shoulder nearly quivering from her barely contained energy. "Believe me, I'm not likely to forget."

He pinched the bridge of his nose in frustration as the only answer pounded through his brain. "My life is complicated in so many ways by virtue of the Medina name. I wish, for your sake, things could be simpler, but they're not." Committed to his new course of action, he skimmed her hair free of her jacket. "I think we should consider an intimate friendship."

Her eyes went wide and unblinking. She sagged back against the desk again, her mouth opening and closing twice before a burst of laughter sliced the air. Wrapping an arm around her stomach, she laughed harder. Her eyes squeezed shut as she shook her head from side to side in obvious disbelief.

"Lilah?" He tucked a knuckle under her chin and turned her face toward him. "This really will be the best option for us to work through this attraction until our lives return to normal."

Her laughter faded, eyes turning somber. "At one time, I may have agreed with you. But it's too late for that now, Carlos."

Disappointment surged through him with more force than he would have expected for his ill-advised plan. He should have approached her sooner. Perhaps she held a grudge that he'd stayed away from her for so long.

Well then, he would dismantle her objections one by one. "I don't agree."

"You don't have all the pertinent information." She straightened to her full height, all of about five feet six inches, bringing her to his shoulder even in her heels. "I'm pregnant. Nearly three months along. And you're the father."

Pregnant?

Shock hit him square in the solar plexus. Followed by disbelief. Then jaded acceptance of her betrayal.

Just when he'd thought he couldn't be any more disillusioned by how easily people could deceive others. A bitter laugh rolled around in his gut and burned a bilious path up his throat.

She crossed her arms under her breasts defensively. "If this is some kind of payback for my laughter earlier, I don't appreciate it. I don't find this in the least amusing."

"Believe me, neither do I." The scars on his back throbbed with a reminder of all he'd lost over twenty-five years ago during his family's escape from San Rinaldo. He told the world the scars had come from a teenage riding accident. That lie was so much more palatable than the truth.

Her mouth went tight, her anger palpable. "This isn't going to make much of a story to tell our child some day."

"Our child? I think not." If anyone had cause to be angry, it was him. "I'm going to give you the benefit of the doubt and assume you're just mistaken about which guy fathered your baby, because I would hate to think you would deliberately try to pass off some other man's kid as mine."

She slapped him, sharp, fast and stingingly hard. "You jackass."

"Excuse me?" he asked, working his jaw from side to side to give himself a chance to weigh his words and tamp down his temper.

"You heard what I said. Believe me, that was the most benign word on my list right now. We may not be…friends…anymore, but I expected better from you than this." She waved her hand through the air as if that could somehow sum up what had transpired between them a minute earlier. "You may be cold, but I thought you were a man of honor."

Scrubbing a hand over his face, he held back the urge to call her on the accusation. She was pregnant—even if it wasn't his. God, the thought rattled him, especially with the leftover surge of hunger for her still cooling in his veins. So much for friends with benefits.

He forced himself to reign in his anger. "Lilah, I'm sorry. But it is *not* my kid."

She tugged her jacket into place again. "I won't force you to love or acknowledge your child. This baby deserves better than that. He or she deserves better than *you*. I've completed my duty in doing the right thing and letting you know. Now you can go straight to hell."

Something in her voice, the intensity of her anger set off warning bells in his brain. She truly thought the child was his when he knew that couldn't be true. If she had the due date wrong by even a couple of weeks, he could see how she might draw that conclusion. Not that he could think of any other man she'd been seeing, but then he'd made a point of avoiding her since their night together.

"Listen closely." He gestured toward her stomach. "That is not my baby, which means you do need to speak to the real father."

A surprise bolt of jealousy shot through him as he fully grasped for the first time the fact she'd slept with someone else close to the time they'd been together. His mind scanned the hospital roster for... Damn it, no. He couldn't go down that path right now.

He forced himself to continue speaking, to make her understand. "You're right that the man deserves to know. And that man can't possibly be me." Not after what had happened to him that night on the run in San Rinaldo. Rebel bullets had killed his mother and nearly killed him while he tried to protect her. Tried. And failed.

He held up a hand to keep her from interrupting—or leaving. "The accident that caused my limp had other physical ramifications as well." Carlos forced himself to say the words he hadn't shared with anyone. "Lilah, I'm sterile."

Two

Lilah had faced her fair share of shockers in her years as a city prosecutor and then administrator at the Tacoma hospital. Certainly learning Dr. Carlos Medina had been hiding his royal lineage had stunned her silly. But his words now beat all other surprising revelations, hands down.

Gripping the edge of the mahogany desk to steady her shaky world, she searched Carlos's face for some sign of what possessed the innately honorable man to deny his own child.

Her hand still stung from her impulsive slap when he'd called her a liar. She hated the momentary loss of control then…and during his kiss earlier. No man affected her this way. She'd fought too long and hard not to be won over so easily like her mother. Yet a simple brush of Carlos's mouth against hers and she'd almost ditched her panties again with this man.

A very virile man who now seemed intent on denying the consequences of their encounter.

"You're sterile?" she repeated, wondering if perhaps she'd heard wrong. She *must* have heard wrong because she carried the living proof of his virility inside her. So either he was wrong or he was a coldhearted liar.

"That's what I said." He shifted his weight to one foot in a manner that to most would look casual. But after years of knowing him, she recognized the subtle way he favored his aching leg and injured back, something he inevitably did when he was under stress.

Carlos Medina was one of those docs with a godlike status around the E.R., the surgeon most likely to pull off a miracle when a gurney wheeled in the impossible. She'd noticed that most people only saw that glow of success and intelligence around him—when they weren't noticing his obvious good looks. Not many people saw past that to detect the fallout of the intense pressure he put on himself. The shifting feet. The tendency to plant his spine against any vertical surface.

Except she could not think of that now. She had too much at stake to get sucked in by all the things she found compelling about this man, not the least of which were these small signs that he was human underneath all that cool professional brilliance.

"Why didn't you say something when we were together that night?" she asked skeptically.

"I didn't see the information as relevant since procreation wasn't on our agenda." His sardonic tone needled at her already tender nerves.

"But you used condoms...even if one failed in the hot tub."

Just thinking of the combustible connection, their total loss of control threatened her balance even now. They'd started in his office, then raced to his home to spend the rest of the night together, awake and making the most of every moonlit minute.

"Safe sex has to do with more than pregnancy," he pointed out practically.

Of course she knew that. She'd freaked when the condom broke, only partially calming down once he'd reassured her he was disease free. Yet in the back of her mind she'd heard the haunting sound of her mother's sobs behind a closed bedroom door. Lilah had been a preteen at the time, but old enough to understand the gist of her parents' fight.

Her father's latest reckless affair had passed along a disease to his wife.

The STD had been treatable, thank heavens, but Lilah had been stunned by how quickly her mother forgave her husband for his infidelity. Again. And again.

Rather than forcing back the memories of her mom, Lilah embraced them for motivation to stand firm now. To push for answers. And to hold Carlos accountable. "This is your child. I don't want money from you and I certainly have no interest in the whole royalty thing. I only want my baby to know his or her father."

"That isn't my baby." His voice echoed with a surety she couldn't miss.

His denial of his own child infuriated her all over again.

"All because of a riding accident when you were a teenager?" She wasn't a doctor but something sounded off in his explanation, in spite of his utter confidence. Still, she couldn't ignore the gravity in his voice, the set serious lines on his aristocratic face.

"The trauma from the accident, coupled with a postsurgical infection, left me sterile. I'm a doctor, in case you've forgotten." He pulled a leather-bound book from the shelves and dropped it on the desk with a resounding thud. "But if you're still in doubt, there's a full chapter in here that discusses such complications. I'll be more than glad to mark the pages for you. The fact remains, though, that your child must have been fathered by someone else."

A shadow smoked briefly through his eyes, something dark and perhaps angry even, but was gone before she could confirm her impression.

If anyone deserved to be mad here, it was her. She wanted to shout her frustration. She *was* telling the father, whether he believed her or not. "Carlos, you aren't listening to me. There is no one else," she explained slowly, carefully, hoping he would hear the truth in her words even if it revealed her vulnerability in wanting only him. "There hasn't been anyone other than you in eight months."

A frown furrowed his forehead, but his silence encouraged her to continue.

"It is absolutely impossible for me to be pregnant with another man's child. And believe me, I *am* pregnant." Her voice shook for the first time. "I've seen the ultrasound. Our baby is alive and well."

The enormity of how much her life had changed so quickly threatened to overwhelm her. She'd always managed to tackle anything life threw her way, whether it be law school at Yale or standing up to a state supreme court judge.

Never had the stakes felt more important than now as she fought for the tiny defenseless life inside her.

Carlos's eyes relayed sympathy and, even worse, a hint of pity. "You really believe this."

"And you really don't."

Finally, she heard and accepted what he'd been saying since she first told him about the baby. She'd anticipated a number of reactions and prepared her rebuttals as carefully as any legal brief. However, she certainly hadn't foreseen this turn of events. Obviously his doctors had been wrong in their diagnosis of Carlos, and his refusal to even consider the possibility, his insistance on believing she'd lied, cut her to the core.

Disillusionment seeped through her veins like a chilly IV flooding through her system. Even though she'd assured herself she didn't need him, she'd hoped for…something…*anything* more than this.

Their kiss a few minutes earlier meant nothing to him. She meant nothing to him. And she needed to numb herself so *he* meant nothing to her.

Lilah pulled in a steeling breath, a trick she'd learned early on to keep her cool when her insides threatened to bubble over with too much unruly emotion. "I've done my part by informing you. A paternity test after the baby is born will confirm I'm telling you the truth. And you're going to feel like a *royal* jerk when you're faced with the proof."

Determined to leave with her pride, Lilah held her head high as she fought back the urge to cry over how terribly the confrontation had gone. While she hadn't expected exuberant cheers by any stretch, she'd hoped for acceptance, followed by stalwart emotional support as they agreed to spell out the practical details of bringing a child into the world. Carlos was a private, reserved man, but he'd always been quietly honorable. Even after his cold shoulder recently, she'd expected better from him than this.

She closed the door with a quiet but firm click, wishing her aching heart was as easy to seal off.

The click of the closing door echoed in his ears, along with the first hints of doubt.

Carlos leaned back against his desk, staring at the space where Lilah had stood seconds before. She'd seemed so certain. In all the years they'd known each other, she'd been an honest woman—a boardroom shark in fighting for the hospital—but always frank and truthful. He admired that about her. For years, in fact, he'd used that admiration of her character to temper his more…primal response to her.

What if…

The possibility of actually being a father rocked his balance far more than the injuries that still caused him to limp to this day. He flattened his clammy palms against the legs of his green hospital scrubs.

While he'd engaged in a number of careful affairs over the years, never had he let a woman truly break through his laser focus on his work. But Lilah was different. He was damn impressed by the way she fought for the hospital, stood up to million-dollar donors and politicians when it came to patients' rights—hell, the way she faced down even him when he dug in his heels too deeply and lost focus on the bigger picture. She had a sharp mind and she wielded it artfully in her profession.

Would she use those same skills against him even now if she thought it would benefit her child?

His father had taught all three of his sons not to trust anyone, anytime. Everybody had a price, including the cousin who had sold out their escape plan. The queen, his mother, Beatriz Medina had died as a result of the ambush that ensued on their way out of San Rinaldo. Carlos had spent his teenage years undergoing surgeries to recover from the gunshot wounds. That he could walk at all was considered a miracle. Doctors told him to be grateful for that much, even if he would never have biological children.

Could he trust Lilah?

As much as he trusted anyone, which wasn't much. God forbid the press should get a hold of this tidbit before he settled the issue. He needed to provide Lilah with concrete proof while keeping matters quiet.

First step, arrange to have the lab run a sperm count test. As much as he balked at the invasion of his privacy, the current results would end this once and for all.

The pesky "what if" smoked through his mind again, the possibility that through some inexplicable miracle her kid turned out to be his after all. Then, he needed to keep Lilah close at hand until the baby could be tested.

Because if against all odds she carried a Medina, nothing would stop him from claiming his child.

Suddenly weary to her toes, Lilah sagged against the closed door. The reception area outside Carlos's office echoed with emptiness, thank goodness. But there was no telling how much longer before his secretary, Wanda, returned to her desk. Her computer already scrolled a screen saver photo of her dozen grinning grandchildren at the Port Defiance Zoo.

Lilah squeezed her eyes closed. The memory of her argument with Carlos rang in her ears. Her belly churned with nausea, unusual for this late in the day. She still battled morning sickness and, no question, upset emotions made it worse. She curved a hand protectively over her stomach, the baby bump barely discernable so early in the pregnancy. Carlos hadn't even noticed when he'd pulled her camisole from her waistband. But she could feel the changes in her body, the swollen tenderness of her breasts, a heightened sense of smell and an insatiable nightly craving for marinated artichokes, a food she had previously hated. While circumstances were far from perfect, she loved her baby with a fierceness that still overwhelmed her at times.

A lock of hair slithered over her cheek and she realized her French twist must be wrecked from Carlos's hands as they'd kissed in his office. Her nipples tingled in lingering awareness of just how fast and high he could stoke desire inside her. She plucked pins from her hair and let the rest slide free around her shoulders, not as professional as she preferred at work, but no doubt better than the sexed-up mess she'd been seconds ago.

For her child's sake, she needed to think rationally rather than with her emotions—or her welling hormones. Carlos obviously believed he was sterile and had only her word that the baby was his. While she wanted to think four years of friendship would have convinced him of her trustworthiness, that clearly wasn't the case.

He was a reserved and private man by nature. His aloofness—hell, his inaccessibility—the past months let her know their friendship wasn't as deep as she'd believed. That she'd been forced to chase him down in the shower to tell him…

Releasing another trapped breath, she refused to get wound up again. She needed to take a step back from him and wait. Time would prove his paternity.

Content she'd regained even ground, Lilah straightened just as the door to the hall opened. She tucked the handful of bobby pins into her jacket pocket and smoothed a hand over her hair to clear any signs of her clench from Wanda's perceptive eyes. There was a reason they called Lilah "The Iron Lady" around this place, and she intended to keep her reputation intact.

The door opened wider, revealing…not Wanda. Lilah tensed for a second, concerned about the press infiltrating the multiple layers of security she'd put in place. Then she recognized one of their newer radiologists, Nancy Wolcott. Her lab coat sported multiple decorative buttons on the lapel. Nancy had once relayed she wore the nonregulation "flair" to put her younger patients at ease. She must be working on the surgical case Carlos was so concerned about.

"Hello, Nancy." Thank heaven her voice stayed steady. "Dr. Medina and I just finished our meeting. I'm sure he will be anxious to hear an update on his young Afghani patient from this afternoon's surgery."

"Oh, I'm not on that case." Smiling hesitantly, the willowy brunette straightened a light-up shamrock pin. "Actually, I'm here on a personal note."

Unease feathered over her. "A personal note?"

"I'm here to meet him for dinner. It's after hours, so

no worries about an administrative sanction. I'm not on
the hospital's clock right now." She shrugged out of her
lab coat and draped it over her arm.

Oh, God, Lilah really didn't like where this conversation was headed, and the timing couldn't have been
worse. She should have seen this coming. Carlos had
never been lacking for dates before his Medina identity
became public. He was a hunky, wealthy doctor, after
all. Albeit a workaholic, temperamental doc. Women
were swarming him now that he'd tacked prince onto
his list of attributes.

She scrambled for something to say and a way to get
out. Fast. "No one can fault your dedication. I know well
how many days you've worked longer shifts when we
needed you. Now if you'll excuse me—"

The younger woman stopped her with a light touch to
the arm. "I should explain. Carlos—Dr. Medina—and
I have been going out for the past few weeks. We've
been careful to keep it under wraps." She adjusted one
of the dozen frames on Wanda's desk. "He really hates
how intrusive the media can be, so we're waiting for the
perfect time for a controlled press release."

No worries about steeling a breath. Nancy Wolcott
had knocked Lilah into next year without even trying.
Carlos, of course, hadn't said a word about it.

And they'd been dating for weeks, not days, not
a onetime outing over coffee. But a relationship that
needed a freaking press release.

Lilah bit back bile. "I hadn't heard."

"I wanted to keep it quiet, too. I know he has a
reputation for keeping relationships light but I think
this might be headed somewhere." Nancy laughed
nervously, seemingly oblivious to the fact she was

gushing. "Perhaps he kept his distance before, back when he had to maintain his royal background. But now that everything's out in the open about his Medina name, he's free to pursue anyone he wants."

Hearing the infatuation in Nancy's voice, Lilah wanted to hate her, to dismiss her like the royalty groupies who'd come out of the woodwork lately. She longed to find fault in someone who'd captured Carlos's interest when a night of sex with her hadn't moved him in even a passing way.

And yet she couldn't be catty. Nancy didn't know about that night with Carlos. No one did.

Furthermore, of every unattached female on staff, this one seemed least likely to be a gold digger or fame seeker. As a part of her job, Lilah knew the history of each employee. Nancy Wolcott was a nice person who very obviously had stars in her eyes over the new man in her life. Who could blame her?

Perhaps a woman who already had Carlos's child swimming around in utero.

A cold ache gelling inside her, Lilah tuned in to the rest of Nancy's lovelorn ramblings.

"I know I'm probably jumping the gun here, but he's such a gorgeous, moody man. A woman can't help but want to touch those inner depths." Nancy pressed a hand to her heart, her eyes fluttering closed as she inhaled.

Lilah wanted to give the woman a good swift kick in her unrealistic expectations about Carlos Medina. Even when he'd dated in the past, she'd seen how emotionally detached the man could be, something that hadn't changed one bit since the whole "son of a deposed monarch" revelation.

Not that she was surprised. There was no such thing

as a fairy-tale ending. Libraries labeled it fiction for
a reason. She'd seen firsthand with her parents how
quickly love soured, how easy it was for a woman to
turn into a pathetic moony-eyed doormat.

Her father had used his job as a Hollywood agent
to seduce countless wannabe starlets. To this day his
wife—Lilah's mother—did her level best to ignore the
indiscretions that messed with her perception of happily
ever after with her hunky, rich dream man. On occasion,
the bimbo of the month set her eyes on a ring or got
angry when the contracts didn't flow in and would
confront the Mrs., forcing her to face her husband's
infidelities.

A fight would ensue. Tears would flow. He would
offer up jewelry or a romantic getaway to "reconnect"
and all would be forgiven until the next time when they
repeated the same dysfunctional cycle all over again—
leaving Lilah with two drawers jam-packed full of tourist
T-shirts brought home by her lovey-dovey parents. In
fact, her parents were on one of their make-up cruises
now, and once they returned she would have to tell them
about the baby.

About Carlos?

Listening to Nancy detail her evening with Carlos
at the symphony, Lilah had to accept that the woman
wasn't blowing anything out of proportion. He really
had asked her out on honest-to-God dates. Not that Lilah
had entertained dreams of such with him. But damn it,
they had slept together. They had been friends before
that. And while he wasn't the warm fuzzy kind, she
deserved better from him than the way he'd treated her
since their one-night stand.

She definitely deserved better than what she'd experienced in his office a few short minutes ago.

Nancy eyed his door warily. "I hope he's not in a bad mood after your confrontation."

Shock jolted her already ragged nerves. Nancy couldn't possibly know about the baby. Had someone been outside the door listening? Wanda, perhaps?

As she calmed down enough to look at Nancy's curious face, she realized the woman was just that—curious. She wasn't shocked or mad, none of the reactions that would be normal if she'd heard rumors that her new "boyfriend" had fathered a child with someone else. "I assume you're referring to the incident in the men's locker room."

"I'm sorry." Nancy pulled up straighter, fidgeting with her logo buttons until they were all cockeyed. "I shouldn't have said anything. I didn't mean to be so chatty."

Lilah eased between her and the exit. "I'm truly curious how you heard this quickly. Please, be frank."

Nancy winced. "I heard in the cafeteria. The buzz is pretty intense as people try to figure out what he did to make you that angry. Bets are being taken for possible reasons."

"And what would those guesses be?"

She nibbled her lip, hesitating for a moment before continuing warily. "Most think you're upset because he blew off that board meeting earlier this week. Others wonder if you're freaking out over him taking on too many pro bono cases. For what it's worth, my money's on the latter. He's such a bighearted man under that gruff exterior."

Lilah gripped the bobby pins in her pocket so tight

they would probably leave holes in her fingers. "Hope you didn't bet the bank on that because you'll lose your life's savings."

If the hospital rumor mill was already churning over one confrontation—granted, a pretty theatrical one—she hated to think how soon her own personal life would be fodder for cafeteria gossip. Good God, she would have to be so much more careful to protect her child's privacy. For the first time it really sunk in that she was carrying a royal child, a person who would be dogged by the press for a lifetime.

Would the news of her child fit on the same press release as Carlos's new girlfriend?

Panic roiled. So much for her decision to opt for an even-keeled "wait and see" attitude. She'd been fooling herself. Her visceral reaction to this woman made it clear too many emotions were involved already.

She needed to keep on fighting rather than letting him roll over her. She would not let her child be hurt by Carlos. She would shield this precious life as best she could from the pain of a father's neglect.

The click of a turning doorknob snapped her attention back to the reception area a second before Carlos's office door opened, the man of the hour filling the frame with his broad shoulders. A flash of surprise raced across his dark eyes.

Anger, frustration and, hell yes, hurt chased through her. Quickly, she stifled the urge to vent the steam building inside her. She'd already made a large enough scene for one day, and she didn't intend to let Carlos know just how deeply he'd wounded her.

That didn't mean she had to balk at making him squirm.

Lilah flicked her loose hair, hair mussed by him during their out-of-control kisses, over her shoulder. "Hello again, Dr. Medina. I was just talking to your new girlfriend."

Three

The shots just kept coming today.

Carlos looked from one woman to the other. How much had Lilah said before he interrupted? Apparently not much since Nancy appeared blessedly oblivious. She was a nice person he'd gone out with a couple of times in hopes of erasing Lilah from his memory.

Nancy was everything he wanted in his personal life. She was intelligent, witty, with common interests and made no demands on his emotions. She should have been perfect for him, except she left him cold. Rather than helping him move on from that colossal mistake, the presence of his "girlfriend" reminded him of just how much every woman paled alongside Lilah.

He'd been planning to break things off with Nancy tonight, even before today's shocking revelation. Continuing to see her when he had unresolved issues with Lilah wasn't fair. Damn shame he hadn't spoken to Nancy a day earlier.

The new radiologist looked from Carlos to Lilah and back again, confusion stamped on her face. "I don't mean to interrupt if you two need to talk business. I can always come back later for our dinner date."

Carlos nodded. "That would be best."

"All righty." She arched up on her toes as if to give him a quick kiss, then paused.

Either she realized such a public display of affection would be inappropriate in the workplace—or she saw Carlos's scowl. Regardless, the woman got the message and pulled away fast.

He caught Lilah's raised eyebrow and added, "Actually, I have an appointment I need to take care of as soon as I check on my patient."

He'd contacted his doctor and the lab about checking his sperm count. He already felt certain of the outcome, but he needed to confirm for Lilah's sake.

And if by some fluke he could father children? Then he would tuck aside his reservations about the way she unsettled his world and launch an immediate campaign to win her over. No half measures, he would be all in, 24/7, until they settled things between them once and for all.

Turning away from Nancy, toward Lilah, he took in her tumbled hair, remembered how it got that way, felt the inevitable kick to his balance. "We will be talking again tomorrow."

Leaving the hospital lab, Carlos walked down the corridor back to his office in a daze. It had been a helluva day. He'd started out operating on a child who reminded him too much of himself, a child caught in the crossfire of war. Before he'd found even five minutes to regain his footing, Lilah had swept aside his shower curtain. Now, his day had ended with the surprise revelation from his own doctor. Not definitive results, by any means, but there was a very slim chance he could father children.

Even the possibility rocked him to the core. He needed time to hole up in his office and plan his next move.

He rounded the corner. Nancy waited beside the door, shuffling from foot to foot while she texted on her cell phone. Apparently she'd been busy while he was gone. She'd changed from her work clothes into a dress—a silky sort of thing for a nice dinner out.

There was no way he could sit through dinner waiting for the right opening to break things off. He needed to make his position clear now. It was the only fair thing to do for Nancy and Lilah.

"Nancy, I'm sorry to have kept you waiting."

"No need to apologize." She tucked her cell phone into her tiny black bag. "I was just telling my best friend about our date tonight."

He winced. "About that." He pushed open his office door. "Let's step into my office so we can talk."

"Oh, um, it's too late in the evening, isn't it?" She scrunched her nose and stayed in the hall. "You need to cancel. I understand. We can go out tomorrow instead. Or how about I cook you dinner—"

"Nancy," he cut her ramble short as gently as possible. "I'm afraid I've given you the wrong impression. This isn't something we should discuss in the hall."

She chewed her lip for a second before smiling, too brightly. She charged into the office ahead of him. He felt bad for misleading her. He'd made a mess of his personal life. He couldn't change the past, but starting now, he could make things right.

As he followed, he decided no more hesitation. No more avoidance. Just as he needed to be clear with Nancy now, he should have settled things with Lilah before.

He wouldn't make the same mistake again. As soon as he finished this confrontation with Nancy, he would go straight to Lilah's—tonight, not tomorrow—and tell her the results of his lab test.

Standing in the open doorway to her penthouse condo, Lilah wished she'd checked the peephole first. But then why hadn't the doorman rang to let her know Carlos was on his way up? Even royalty shouldn't be given a free pass into her building.

Granted, she wouldn't have sent Carlos away, but she would have liked a second to prepare herself before facing him again.

Corridor sconces bathed him in a halogen glow as he waited. Moisture from the light rain clung to his hair and glinted on the hint of silver at his temples. Too easily, she could envision him damp from his shower earlier. Except now he wore clothes. His long trench was open, revealing his gray suit, red tie trekking down his chest the way her fingers itched to mimic.

The hall echoed with intimate silence, everyone else tucked in for the night inside their units in the restored waterfront building. Carlos had been here in the past for informal gatherings, drop-ins and dinner parties, but always with others. Never alone.

Totally alone. Like now.

She gripped the brass doorknob tighter. "I thought you said we would be speaking tomorrow."

The scent of the salty outdoor air clung to him, teasing her nose.

"My appointment took care of itself faster than I expected." Palm flattened to the door frame, he looked past her shoulder into her condo. "We should step inside."

Even fully covered in silky sleep pants and matching green paisley top, she was too aware of the nighttime, her PJs and *him*. "It's polite to ask to be invited in rather than demand."

His jaw flexed with irritation. "Let's stop with the word games. We have important business to discuss."

Of course, he was right. She just resented that he'd caught her unawares, dictating the time and manner of their meeting. "Come inside, then. But don't get too comfortable. It's been a long—" *disappointing* "—day. I'm tired."

Careful to step well clear of him, she pressed her back against the hall rather than risk an accidental brush of her body and his. His uneven gait thudded against the freshly restored hardwood floors as he walked deeper into her condominium. She loved her two-bedroom haven full of character from the whitewashed brick walls to the soaring ceiling with exposed beams and a loft office. A wall of windows revealed the twinkling lights of the Tacoma skyline, historic Foss Waterway and a fog-ringed mountain in the distance.

Shrugging out of his trench coat, Carlos stopped just shy of her burgundy sofa, half in, half out of her place, much like he kept himself from committing to any people, emotions, relationships. "About Nancy—"

She cut him off with the wave of her hand. "I don't care who you date." And maybe if she kept saying it often enough, she would believe it. "That's your business and has nothing to do with us. We were never a couple. You and I have nothing more to say to each other outside of hospital business until after the paternity test."

"Nancy and I are not an item, never were," he ignored her final jab, sticking to the point he seemed determined to press. "We had a couple of casual dates, and I'd already decided to break things off before today."

"How convenient, but still not relevant." She padded closer to him, her bare feet whispering along the cool, bare flooring. "If that's all you came to say, then we're done."

She pointed to the door.

He flung aside his trench to rest on the back of a striped chair and clasped her wrist in a big but gentle grip. Silently, slowly, *deliberately,* he folded her arm back against her chest, which brought him closer to her. His eyes turned smoky with intensity….

And focused on her mouth.

Her heart somersaulted in her chest. "Don't even go there, Carlos," she warned, but didn't pull away. "Any urge to kiss you evaporated once you refused to believe me about the pregnancy."

Teasing his thumb along her speeding pulse, he stilled her again with his eyes. "I came here to tell you that I'm willing to entertain the possibility this could be my baby."

The sensual tug, the raspy allure of his callused fingers on her skin sidetracked her, delaying her brain from absorbing his words for three, needy heartbeats.

Then awareness faded from her body as his words

penetrated, followed by realization of the reason for his surprise visit. She leaned nearer, her breasts so close to his chest a simple deep inhale could skim her tingling nipples against him.

She kept her breathing shallow, even as she lowered her voice into a husky whisper sure to heat his exposed neck. "Got a sperm count check, did you? That was quick."

A fleeting dry smile twitched his mouth. "It helps having connections in the medical world."

Confirmation of her suspicion didn't make her feel one bit better. He wasn't here because he had a change-of-heart decision to trust her word. He'd gotten his proof. While she understood on an intellectual, practical level, she was currently feeling anything but sensible.

Let alone amenable.

"How nice for you." She wrenched her wrist from his grip, wrapping her arms around herself and stalking to the window wall. "What a shock it must have been that you still have swimmers."

"How nice that you find my medical history so amusing."

"I don't find any of this at all funny. Particularly your insinuations about my honesty earlier." She half looked back at him over her shoulder. "Have you let your new girlfriend know?"

Ouch, she hadn't meant to bring up the whole Nancy issue again and sound—God forbid—jealous. She looked away quickly before he could see any betraying emotions on her face.

His footsteps echoed behind her, closer, the sound and feel of him too familiar. "I told you already." He stroked back her hair from her ear. "I broke things off with her."

Goose bumps rose on her skin, twinkling boat lights on the water blurring as everything faded but the sound of his breathing, the light skim of his fingers. Good God, his surgeon hands had such a capacity for minute movements, meticulous attentiveness until he turned even an inch of her shoulder into a volatile erogenous zone.

"Well, she should know you can still—"

Her words hitched up short on her next breath, heat flooding through her body and pooling low. The crisp scent of him—night air and ocean breeze—drew nearer, stronger, until she flattened her hand against the cool windowpane to steady herself.

He cupped her shoulders in broad, careful hands and turned her to face him. "She does not need to be informed."

Did that mean they weren't sleeping together or that he'd been more careful? She tried not to care about the answer, hating that he had such power over her feelings. The way her temperature spiked when she simply looked at him, the sensation of the room shrinking to just the two of them. All too easily she could lose sight of how important it was to keep her head clear.

Shifting her focus from herself to her child, she asked, "What did the doctor have to say?"

His fingers slid down the length of her arms before he tucked his hands into his trouser pockets. "I can give you the lengthy technobabble about motility and counts if you wish. But while chances are very low I can father a child," he swallowed hard, "the chance does exist."

That simple slow swallow spoke emotional volumes

from such an aloof man. Sympathy for him stirred against her will. What a shocker this day must have been for him on a number of levels, which didn't excuse the way he'd betrayed their friendship over the past few weeks with his aloof behavior. But still, the hurt and disappointment eased at having him backtrack. Now, finally, they could make plans for their baby.

She chewed her lip, tasting toothpaste from her earlier attempt to brush away the persistent memory of his kiss. "I realize this must be a big surprise for you—"

"My feelings are irrelevant," he charged over her, his face set again in a mask she'd seen him don during especially taxing surgeries. "I spoke with a GYN colleague and we can have a chorionic villus sampling done in your twelfth to fourteenth week of pregnancy to determine paternity."

An early paternity test? He *still* doubted her? So much for sympathetic leanings on her part.

Anger starched up her spine again vertebrae by vertebrae. "Fine. You've said what you came here for—"

"Actually, I haven't finished."

"Well, good for you. However, I've had more than enough of your company for one day."

"That's my point. Today hasn't gone well for either of us. And regardless of how that test comes out, we're going to be tied to each other, whether through the pregnancy or through work. I'm assuming you have no intention of changing jobs and neither do I."

"That hasn't stopped you from being a jerk since December." She jabbed him in the chest with her pointer. "Other people—" *like Nancy* "—may be willing to put up with your moodiness because you were a hospital legend even before you turned out to be some kind of royalty, but I happen to think that excuses nothing."

"You're absolutely correct on all counts." His angular face creased with the first smile she'd seen from him in so long, longer than she could remember. The power of it was so much stronger than it should be.

Her arm fell to her side. "Pardon me?"

"You heard me." He stroked back a lock of her hair then withdrew his hand before she could object. "You're right. I've been a—what did you say earlier?—a jackass."

She sank onto her sleek red sofa, trying to process this latest surprise turn from him, tough to do when he scattered her thoughts with a simple touch or heated look. "What brought you around to my way of thinking?"

Settling onto the gray-and-white striped chair beside her, he leaned forward, elbows on his knees—closer to her. "Actually, seeing you and Nancy in the office together. I should have given our impetuous night together some closure before moving on."

Stunned anew, she bit her tongue, afraid if she spoke, his surprising chattiness would dry up as quickly as it started.

"I still stand by what I said the morning after we were together." He stared at her intently, his linked hands so close to her legs if she even twitched, they would make contact. "I shouldn't have let things go that far between us, but I also shouldn't have assumed things could return to normal either."

She refrained from mentioning the past months had brought anything but a return to normal. He'd become even more of a workaholic than normal, leaving not even a free half hour for a simple shared coffee as they'd done in the past. Although apparently he'd found time for dates with Nancy Wolcott.

Damn, that green-eyed monster was a tenacious beast. "What is your point?"

"We have about a week's window before the paternity test to find even ground. I propose that we make the most of it."

Suspicion prickled. Could he be making a move on her because of that kiss? While she might have caved to the temptation of that passionate clench a few weeks ago, now that she knew about the baby she needed to be more cautious. "Make the most of it in what way?"

"Let's both take a week of vacation. We leave Washington and work behind to focus 24/7 on clearing the air."

Except he never took time off. Ever.

His offer to step away from the hospital rocked her, and also made her wonder if he could actually be serious. Her own calendar was packed solid. However, he had a point about the future. And she already knew how that paternity test would turn out. This truly could be her only chance to resolve her feelings for Carlos. Her only chance to protect her heart for the many times she would have to face him in the coming years.

"A week off from the hospital," she parroted, needing confirmation even if she didn't know what she would do once she got it. "Just you and me?"

"That's what I said." He nodded curtly, a lock of hair sliding across his forehead. He worked such insane hours he even missed regular haircuts.

"What about your patients? And what about the little girl you operated on this afternoon?"

"My part in her medical plan is complete. As for my

other cases, everything can be handled by doctors on staff."

Heaven knows there were plenty of physicians who owed him for the times he'd stepped in for them and countless holidays spent on call so they could be with their families.

Still, she didn't quite trust he would simply drop everything in Tacoma. There must be a catch. "Where would we go?"

"How about Colorado? My family owns a house there."

Panic tickled. "Who else lives there?"

"No one. It's a resort property. It's empty now and completely at our disposal."

Alone? Just the two of them? While she wasn't ready for a meet-the-parents moment, she also wasn't sure total isolation with her hot onetime lover was such a brilliant idea either.

Although memories of what a jerk he'd been today could provide plenty of protection. Then she thought of the tiny life growing inside her and knew she didn't have any choice. Certainly this was a surprise baby at a time when she'd begun to wonder if perhaps motherhood wasn't in the cards for her. But from the moment she'd seen the heart fluttering on the ultrasound, she'd known she would do anything, absolutely *anything* for her child.

Including spend seven tempting days alone with Carlos Medina.

Outside Lilah's condo building, Carlos closed the door on his Mercedes SUV and hooked his arm over the steering wheel.

Puget Sound stretched out beyond his windshield, hazy through the misty rain. Through the tinted windows, he soaked in the sight, gaining some mystical comfort from the light roll of waves.

Water locales drew him, his brothers as well, likely because it reminded them of their island homeland of San Rinaldo. His middle brother, Duarte, had left their father's fortress to scoop up seaside investment resorts before settling in Martha's Vineyard. Antonio, the youngest Medina son, had been drawn to the warmer climate of Galveston Bay, where he'd become a shipping magnate. Ironically, even their half sister, Eloisa, spent most of her life in Pensacola, Florida, before settling with her new husband in Hilton Head, South Carolina.

He could only conclude that the shores called to something centuries old in their genetics. The scientist inside him didn't make so much as a peep in protest of the illogical thought. He felt the proof surging through his veins. Only once had he felt anything as strong—the night he'd spent with Lilah. The past few months he'd been fighting the temptation to lose himself in her again. He'd tried to move on.

Today had proved his failure on that front all too well. Now, he had a full week with her. Seven days to level things with her, setting the course for the rest of his life. He would either tie her to him so they could parent their child or work her out of his system so he could walk away if she'd lied about the baby's paternity.

To accomplish his goal, he needed to get her away from here, in a setting under his control, no surprises from work or the press.

He fished his phone from the inside of his suit coat

and thumbed speed dial for his brother Duarte, the next in line after him for their father's tarnished crown.

Before the second ring even finished, his brother's voice came across speakerphone, "Speak to me, brother."

Carlos didn't bother apologize for calling late, even more so for Duarte who was three hours ahead on East Coast time. He and his siblings didn't speak every other day by any means, but when one called, they dropped everything else.

"Just calling to check up on our father." Enrique Medina had been near death for over six months from a failing liver. "How's he doing?"

"Still holding on. He's tough. I'm starting to wonder if maybe he will beat this after all."

Carlos knew the poor odds too well from a medical perspective so he opted to switch the subject instead. "I may be coming for a visit in a few days. I'm not going to say anything to him until I'm sure—" *sure if the baby is mine* "—but want to give you the heads-up."

"Just name the time and Kate and I will be there."

The sound of rustling sheets and a sleepy female mumble echoed through the phone line. Duarte was engaged to a reporter, a surprisingly illogical choice, especially given his brother's usual methodical ways. But he'd fallen and fallen hard. There'd been no doubting that when Carlos had seen him with her at Antonio's wedding a couple of months ago.

Normally, he balked at returning to the isolated compound where they'd relocated after escaping San Rinaldo, so many bad memories linked to their new "home." The island complex had been outfitted with a top-notch physical rehab center, where he'd spent most of his teenage years. His brothers had been his only friends during those days, and even so with the surgeries and recoveries, there hadn't been much time to learn about relationships.

Although he felt anything but "brotherly" around Lilah.

His gaze shifted from the shoreline to the historic brick complex housing Lilah's restored condo. "I may be bringing someone with me."

"Care to share details?"

"Not yet."

Looking up to the tenth floor—the penthouse—he could swear he saw Lilah outlined in her window for a second before she clicked off the light. Preparing for bed? He hardened at the thought of peeling off her clothes. Lowering her onto the mattress. Imprinting himself on her. And hoping like hell that baby was his so he could take Lilah again and again, and damn the consequences to his carefully constructed world.

He hauled his attention off her condo and back to the conversation. "She and I are going to spend some time together over the next few days while I check on a couple of Father's holdings."

Enrique owned investment properties around the U.S., and even a few outside the States. Savvy financial purchases, yes, but they'd also been bought to create more confusion over where the deposed king had settled.

Enrique had already begun parceling off parts of his estates to each of his sons. While Carlos couldn't have cared less about any inheritance, he saw the wisdom in protecting the family interests if for no other reason than he could donate additional monies to the charities of his choice. He could make it possible for more children to receive the surgeries they needed, to have a chance at enjoying their youth in a way he couldn't.

However, he refused to wallow in self-pity or bemoan all he'd lost. He preferred to charge forward and take control of the future, and normally he succeeded. Except on a day like today, the past, the injury, the acute cut of loss, were thrown in his face in an unavoidable way. Flexing his aching leg, he pushed back the temptation to imagine the face of an infant, his child.

God help Lilah if she'd lied to him.

And God help him if she hadn't. Because then he couldn't seal himself off from the past with a solitary existence any longer.

"Duarte, I'll keep in touch. Sleep well, my brother."

He disconnected the call, his eyes drawn up to the darkened penthouse where Lilah slept. Alone for tonight, but not much longer.

Tomorrow, he would begin his campaign to get back in her good graces with a trip to the family lodge in Vail, Colorado. Hopefully a few intimate nights by the fire would melt her walls and burn away the cold fist that had stayed lodged in his chest since the morning she'd left his bed.

Four

Lilah had been running full-out since the minute she'd rolled out of bed this morning. The day had been jam-packed with continuous phone calls to the hospital in attempts to clear her schedule for a week while she packed, dressed and prepped her condo for her reckless getaway with Carlos.

Now, ensconced in his limousine on the way to the airport, the enormity of what she'd done washed over her until her fingers dug deeply into the supple leather seat.

Late-day rain pattered on the limo's clear sunroof, streaks muting the already cloudy sky. Much like her nerves, it made her apprehension all the worse. She could barely believe she'd agreed to this crazy plan of his, an impulsive idea so unlike the normally methodical man. Perhaps that's why she'd agreed. He must be every bit as thrown by life as she was right now to even suggest such a plan.

Although he looked anything but rattled as he checked updates from the hospital on his phone. While he may have transferred his cases to another physician, he obviously hadn't off-loaded the concerns from his mind. Intense concentration furrowed his brow, his dark, chocolate-brown eyes taking on a distant look as he stared out the window, his mind obviously still on his young patients.

Even in casual jeans and a black cable sweater, he was one hundred percent in charge. His dedication softened her heart, which kept her from tapping on the privacy window and asking the chauffer to take her home.

Today, Carlos was particularly involved in checking up on his very young patient from yesterday's surgery. The deep, low rumble of Carlos's bass filled the roomy limo with his exotic Spanish accent. Even with the blast of the vehicle's heater, the chill of the damp day seeped into her and made her ache to cuddle into the heat of the warm-blooded—undoubtedly hot—man beside her.

Her cashmere blend dress suddenly itchy against her oversensitive skin, she scratched the back of her neck, tucking her hand under the concealed zipper.

Carlos clipped his phone to his jeans and turned his attention toward her. "I assume everything is fine for you to travel. I didn't even think to ask last night and I should have. My apologies."

His concern touched her. "I spoke with my doctor this morning to be sure. And yes, travel is fine or I wouldn't be here. I packed my vitamins and am taking care of myself."

"Would you like something to drink? Some spring

water?" He gestured to the gleaming silver minifridge. "A light snack?"

"No, thank you." Her hands were trembling so much she would likely spill it anyway. "Maybe later."

"Any morning sickness?" he asked in his oh-so-familiar physician tone.

"Some," she responded slowly, curious as to his grilling. "The nausea's not pleasant, to say the least, but tolerable."

Suspicion niggled as she wondered if his questions had more to do with relegating her to a safe, distant role of patient rather than genuine concern for her, for their baby.

Hurt grated against her already ragged nerves. "Why the sudden interest in this pregnancy? Are you searching for clues that I'm not as far along as I say? Is that what this trip is really all about? You must realize a person can travel 'til nearly the eighth month."

He stretched his arm along the back of her seat, inches away from encircling her shoulders. The scent of him mingled with leather and new car smell. "Let's not begin a fight. This time together is about finding common ground."

While he was right on that point, resentment still simmered. "How can you simply shut down unpleasantness in a snap? I'm not accustomed to compartmentalizing my life that way."

"How then do you function during a crisis at the hospital?" he retorted without missing a beat.

"That's different." Wasn't it? "That's a unique moment in time. Life isn't one continual crisis."

He grunted noncommittally. "If you say so."

Was her pregnancy being relegated to crisis level?

So, then, what was this time with her through his eyes? Damage control? "Surely you must have some way to relax, making time to lower those thick walls you put around yourself."

A one-sided grin creased his cheek but never reached his eyes. "Letting down your guard is highly overrated, not to mention dangerous."

Dangerous? A pall settled over their conversation. "Because you're royalty?"

Which meant her child was a royal as well. She resisted the urge to lean back into the safety, the protection, of the hard-muscled beam of his arm.

He teased a lock of her loose hair. "Ah, you remember my Medina roots after all."

"That's a strange thing to say."

His head tipped to the side, his smoky eyes raking her with an appreciative gaze. "I appreciated the way you didn't treat me differently after the news story broke about my family's hidden identity."

The compliment soothed her raw nerves and also made her wonder. "Is that why things changed between us, why you made a move on me at the party?"

Hesitating, he scrubbed a hand over the five o'clock shadow already peppering his strong, square jaw. "In part. You were the one person who didn't want to talk about San Rinaldo."

Because she'd seen how people suddenly treated him differently. She'd noticed how uncomfortable the kowtowing made him. And, quite frankly, she'd found his work at the hospital to be infinitely more admirable than any royal fortune or regal bloodlines.

That he preferred anonymity to media attention impressed her all the more. "Thank you, Carlos."

"For what?"

"For telling me that." For helping reassure her going with him now was the right thing to do. She needed these insights as to what made Carlos tick. She needed this trip.

She needed *him*.

Her eyes fell to his mouth, a strong masculine slash that could turn so tender on her bared body. Memories flooded her mind of the first time he'd kissed her at the hospital fundraiser, standing out on the balcony with a romantic flurry of snow casting a crystal sheen on everything around her. The second Carlos's mouth had covered hers, she'd been warmed to her toes.

Like the heat rekindling in her veins now.

It would be so easy to lean into him, to recapture that magical connection. What a mixed blessing these feelings were. What she felt with him surpassed anything she'd experienced before, but that meant all other men paled in comparison. She ached from wanting something so wrong for her. They still had so much left unsettled. He still didn't trust her.

But an answering blaze flared in his eyes.

The patter of the rain closed out everything but the sound of their breathing, the brush of his thigh along hers as he shifted. Carlos dipped his head silently, close but not near enough to make contact. Clearly he was letting her know he wanted to kiss her every bit as much as she wanted him, but was leaving the next move up to her. Her thudding heartbeat echoed in her ears as the moment ticked out.

Did she dare say to hell with it all? Make the most of this time together before the baby complicated matters further? Indulge herself in the unsurpassed pleasures she'd found with Carlos?

The spacious limousine became full of possibilities. She could straddle his lap and take control with ease, thanks to the dress she wore. Or she could lean back and invite him to stretch his muscular length over her. The tingling need skipping through her veins gathered between her legs until she pressed her knees together against the sweet ache.

The limo slowed, turning off the highway and signaling the nearing end of their drive. A flush burned up her face as she realized how close she'd come to throwing herself at Carlos. She inched toward her door, tugging the hem of her sapphire cashmere dress securely over her knees until it touched the tops of her black leather boots.

Carlos angled away and back to his side, supple leather seat crackling softly under the give and shift of bodies. Just as it would have sounded had she acted on her desire to have him here and now. Every sound, each nuance, felt so intimate in light of the time they would be spending together.

The luxury vehicle rocked gently as the car slid to a stop. They'd arrived at the airport, and while they would leave the confines of the car soon, they were simply exchanging the solitude of the limo for the seclusion of a private jet.

Before she could stem her fluttering nerves, the driver opened the passenger door, holding an umbrella over her head to protect her from the light drizzle. She swung her feet out, her eyes sweeping the small, private airport, a simple one-story red brick building with four hangars and a lone runway. A Learjet swooshed upward into the murky sky.

A pair of businessmen with matching black umbrellas rushed toward the covered walkway. A family of four huddled underneath the shelter as an SUV rumbled toward them. Lilah couldn't tear her eyes from the frazzled family tableau. While the father snagged his son from stomping galoshes through a puddle, the mother scooped up a toddler in a yellow duck raincoat that swallowed the child so fully it was impossible to determine gender.

Her hand gravitated to her stomach and she swallowed back a betraying sigh. But it was difficult to stem the flood of hopeful images, especially when Carlos had already made a first step toward opening up.

Warily hopeful, she shifted her attention to the tiny terminal where they would officially launch their journey. A woman stood by the door with a tomato-red umbrella. Actually an umbrella with a tomato stem on top, with a familiar female waiting and waving underneath the bright shelter.

Lilah stumbled on the curb.

It couldn't be….

But a closer look confirmed her suspicion. None other than Nancy Wolcott, Carlos's supposedly "ex" girlfriend, waited at the airport entrance.

Holy hell.

Wincing, Carlos scrubbed his bristly jaw. What was Nancy Wolcott doing here at the private airport?

And clearly waving at them.

Her presence didn't make sense. He had made himself clear, in a polite fashion. They were both adults. She'd seemed to understand. Yes, she'd seemed disappointed and expressed regret, but not overly so.

He took the offered umbrella from the chauffer and slid under alongside Lilah. Her gasp let him know she'd seen the woman too and was none too happy. The timing couldn't have been worse. All the progress he'd made on the ride over was blasted to bits now. His body was still strung taut with desire and images of how easy it would have been to lean Lilah back on the leather seats….

He cut the thought short and focused on the mess at hand. Planting a hand on the small of Lilah's back, he steered her with him, toward the airport entrance. Toward the waiting train wreck.

"Yoo-hoo," Nancy called, her waving intensifying, raindrops sliding from the umbrella faster in her animation. "Over here!"

He shot a quick assessing glance at Lilah and found her lips thin and tight with irritation, her boots clicking in a snappy fast pace he recognized as angry. He'd heard the same stomping rhythm before as she left a particularly frustrating board meeting. Now was not the time to ponder the reason he knew her well enough to read the mood of her footsteps.

Stopping beside Nancy, Carlos reined in his own frustration over the woman's surprise arrival.

Nancy's smile widened. "What perfect timing. I'm so glad I caught you before you left, Carlos."

Lilah stayed silent, but Carlos had different plans. There were important details to learn before he sent Nancy on her way. "How did you know to come here? And what time?"

"It's not a state secret, is it? I just wanted to tell you goodbye." She stared at Lilah curiously, closing her umbrella slowly and shaking it dry. "I didn't realize the two of you would be traveling together. You didn't tell me that yesterday, Carlos."

Blown away by the way she'd shown up here when he'd made it clear yesterday they both needed to go their separate ways, he wondered how he could have misread Nancy. Not that he'd really known her well when he asked her out.

What had made him gravitate to Nancy so soon after his time with Lilah? On the surface, the women were total opposites in many ways. Which made him wonder if perhaps he'd chosen Nancy for just that reason.

Had that one night he'd shared with Lilah sent him running scared? That possibility rocked his world in a way it would take some serious time to process.

Carlos stepped aside for the pair of businessmen passing. "Nancy, quite frankly, I prefer to keep details of my travels low-key and private."

"Of course." The woman nodded quickly, clutching her shiny red umbrella closer. "I only want to speak to you alone for a few minutes, you know, about what we discussed at the hospital before you left." She glanced at Lilah pointedly.

Before Carlos could insist she stay, Lilah hitched her purse higher on her shoulder and said, "I need to make some work calls. If you'll excuse me."

"No. Don't go." He clasped Lilah's arm while keeping the other, unpredictable woman clearly in his sights. Who knew what she might do next? "Nancy, I'm sorry, but let's not make this awkward for anyone. There's nothing more to say. I believe I covered everything yesterday."

He kept his voice firm and no-nonsense while

working not to be outright cruel. But she needed to understand there could be nothing more.

Nancy's face froze, her grin turning brittle. "You're right. I apologize for wanting to send you off on a nicer note." Her icy smile included Lilah now. "Have a safe business trip."

Tomato umbrella swooping up and sending a fresh shower of water outward, Nancy raced out into the parking lot toward her hatchback. Regret bit at him that he hadn't handled things better with her the day before. He hadn't meant to be a coldhearted bastard, but…damn. Maybe he should have thought of that before they'd dated.

Annoyed with himself and with Nancy, Carlos watched to make sure she got into her car and left. Once her car cleared the parking lot, he turned to Lilah again.

Frowning, she swept water from her wool coat and the hem of her cashmere dress. "Have many more groupies waiting to waylay us before we board?"

Instinctively, he reached for his phone. "I'm more concerned with how she found out we're here and how much more she knows about our travel plans."

A call to his family's security team was in order. As much as he wanted to launch his quest to seduce Lilah, nothing could take precedence over her safety. Once they were secured on the plane, he would turn his attention to discovering how Nancy Wolcott unearthed his travel itinerary and just how much she knew.

Jet engines humming softly, Lilah unbuckled from her seat for a better view out the window at the night sky. Anything to distract her from what she really wanted to study. Carlos, reclined and sleeping an arm stretch away, kept stealing her attention.

Before they'd even left the ground, he'd been working his phone assigning some security team—apparently he kept one on retainer?—to figure out how Nancy had tracked them to the airport. A security team, for crying out loud. Once his "people" had been given their marching orders, Carlos had fallen asleep in a blink, a skill he'd picked up catching catnaps during long shifts at the hospital.

How could he look so familiar but seem so different out of their medical realm? She wasn't a millionaire, but she was financially secure in her own right. She'd also grown up with her fair share of glitz due to her father's connections to the Hollywood scene—although he'd been known to live beyond his means, which led to a feast-and-famine lifestyle for his family.

Still, even her own experience of brushing elbows with the rich and famous hadn't come close to the scope of influence she was only just beginning to see Carlos wielded. While she couldn't deny Carlos attracted her physically, she refused to be swayed by the wealth of his world of secretive itineraries, plush limousines and private jets. And a very determined female radiologist whose behavior bordered on stalking.

Lilah gripped the leather armrests tighter. Seeing Nancy Wolcott waiting and waving had provided a hefty reminder for how little she knew about Carlos. And how important it was to gauge her moves carefully.

She looked away from the starkly handsome man snoozing across from her and turned her attention to the sleeping world of tiny lights below. If only things were as straightforward as they'd once been with Carlos, just a few shorts months ago before that fateful Christmas fundraiser. Back during a time when she'd been able to rein in her wayward attraction to the brooding surgeon who haunted her dreams.

Carlos didn't believe dreams came only in black-and-white. His always felt far more vivid than that as the real world mixed with the slumber sphere. Perhaps because he'd slept lightly for as long as he could remember.

As a child, he'd been taught to stay on guard against threats to him as heir to the throne. Then he'd been denied REM sleep by the claws of pain recovering from the shooting. And, finally, he'd needed to stay on alert for his patients.

Right now, his dream mixed with the recycled plane oxygen blending the scent of Lilah with some kind of pine air freshener…taking him back to that night at the hospital fundraiser nearly three months ago….

Lighted pine trees decorating the sprawling hospital conference room, Carlos stirred his sparkling water, refusing anything stronger until the fundraiser finished. And then, just call him Scrooge, because all bets were off.

Christmas meant celebrations and special family moments to most people. Carlos preferred a bottle of memory-numbing bourbon to get through the holidays.

But first, he had to fulfill work obligations.

He tugged at his tux tie absently. He hated the damn thing, but his presence was required at the formal event. Wealthy contributors liked to rub elbows with the doctors who used their money to save lives.

Apparently he was the celebrity of the hour since news of his Medina heritage had broken. He would give over his entire inheritance if it would get him out of this diamond-studded circus. Even his family's fortune wouldn't be enough for him to bid farewell to fundraiser dog and pony shows.

His back hurt like hell after a relentless day of surgery after surgery. Seeing Lilah offered the first distraction in an otherwise crappy day. Her auburn hair was swept up in a bundle of loose curls rather than her regular tight twist. During office hours she wore button-up power suits, linen and layers that left him imagining peeling each piece off. Now, however, there was much more of her creamy skin on display. Not in an overt way, but enough that his fingers curled in his pockets from restraint.

The gold silk gown wrapped around her curves, giving her a Grecian goddess appeal. Beaded details glinted from the chandelier's light. The luminescent glow of her bared shoulders, however, outshone everything else.

She smiled at him, leaned toward the person she'd been speaking to—excusing herself?—and walked toward him. Silky fabric swirled around her legs with each graceful glide.

For four years he'd resisted the attraction. Persistent. Ever present. Increasingly painful appeal.

Tonight, with memories of that final, ill-fated Christmas in San Rinaldo pounding in his head like the unrelenting bullets that had killed his mother, his ears ringing, ringing, ringing, he didn't have the willpower to resist....

Five

The airplane phone rang and rang and rang, jarring Lilah from her dazed stare out the window at the distant mountain peaks below. She started to walk across to answer the phone before the jangling disturbed Carlos's catnap, but he bolted upright in the reclined lounger and snagged the receiver.

"Speak," he barked into the phone in his normal gruff fashion.

Some parts of his blunt personality were still all too familiar.

He scrubbed a hand over his eyes, his groggy look clearing in a flash as he transformed back to the alert surgeon, the intense man she knew from work. He returned his seat to the upright position. After a few clipped responses of "good," "excellent" and "keep me posted" rumbling from him, he disconnected the call.

Unbuckling, he stood with an almost disguised wince and started toward her. "Apparently Nancy figured out my plans to fly out from a note Wanda had jotted on her desk. If that's the case, then Nancy knows nothing more about our travel plans than the airport location."

Lilah thumbed the brass casing around the window, polishing a nonexistent smudge. "It's a relief to know we don't have to worry about Nancy waiting for us when we land in Vail."

"We can move on to the vacation part of our plans with a clear mind." He glanced at his watch. "Sorry to have napped so long. You must be hungry. Our steward can bring a light snack or supper even. Whatever you wish, I'll make it happen."

"How about a double bacon cheeseburger with a mint chocolate chip milkshake?" she asked, only half joking. She was learning just how tenacious pregnancy cravings can be.

He reached for the call button. "I'll see what he can put together."

Resting her hand on his wrist, she stopped him. "I was kidding. Really, I'm not hungry yet. I just need to stretch my legs. The seats are fabulous—" as was everything on this top-of-the-line private craft "—but my back hurts if I sit too long."

His brow furrowed as he studied her. Muscular shoulders encased in warm black wool called to her fingers until everything else faded. Her mouth went dry. Carlos's gaze fell to her mouth and she couldn't stop her tongue from teasing along her lips. His nostrils flared with awareness.

She and he had a sensual connection, without question. But there was no emotional connection of any substance. Right? As long as she remembered that, she should be able to protect her heart.

His hand settled at the base of her spine, as if already testing her resolve. She started to inch away, but he pressed ever so slightly, ever so perfectly, against the spot that ached. Again, she reminded herself the physical was different from the emotions. Why should she deny herself the comfort—the undiluted pleasure—of his touch?

His fingers circled with deepening pressure and she sighed. A hint of a moan hitched a ride on the gusty breath making its way up her throat.

While massaging in increasingly larger circles, he reached past her to slide open the shade further to improve the view of the clusters of city lights below. "How much does your back hurt?"

"Just a little...right there."

His intuitive touch gave her pause as she realized just how he knew what to do. He lived in constant pain without a complaint.

Straightening, she inched aside. "It's nothing I can't handle."

He followed, his hands never leaving her body. "There's no need for you to handle it all. I'm trying to be nice, so stop arguing. Doctor's orders."

"Okay, then." She began to offer to rub his back in return and then almost gasped.

An urge to laugh followed, chased by a bittersweet sense of how special this would have been had it happened the morning after they'd been together. Or if he'd apologized nicely yesterday for being a jerk these past months, providing a perfectly logical explanation for his behavior.

But she wasn't whimsical. She was practical. Therefore she would enjoy this blasted backrub to the fullest. It was about the physical, nothing to do with her emotions.

Talking, however, would help keep her grounded more in reality and less in the sensual play of his fingers working tension from knotted muscles. "We haven't gotten to talk since boarding. Is the plane yours?"

"My family owns controlling interest in a small charter company," he answered softly from behind her, his subtle accent curling around each word and into her. "It's an investment that also enables us to fly wherever we wish with minimal discussion of our plans."

"No one knows your itinerary."

"That's the idea. I've been able to lead a relatively normal life at the hospital since my identity became public. You run a tight ship and I appreciate that. But out in the real world, I need to be careful."

Which explained why he was especially concerned to find Nancy waiting for them. Her shoulders rose with tension. He skimmed upward to cup them, rubbing until they lowered again. Relaxation radiated through her as he became some kind of medical magician.

"That's better. Just let go," he said, his mouth closer to her ear this time.

Unable to resist, she soaked in the heat of his breath against her neck, inhaled the peppermint scent of his toothpaste. What would it be like if he were telling her to "just let go" while they were doing other, more intimately pleasurable things?

She dragged her attention off his command in her ear and scrambled for something coherent to say.

"You've got a family-owned air taxi service for the rich and famous." She traced the teakwood encircling the portal, brass edging gleaming. She'd ridden with her father in similar crafts as a kid. Of course, thinking about her dad was worse than thinking of Nancy.

"Actually," Carlos's thumbs pressed between her shoulder blades with intuitive precision that sent waves of pleasure radiating outward, "Enrique—my father— diversified the company a few years ago so that when the planes are not in use for the needs of our family and our associates, they are used on call for search-and-rescue emergencies."

"Your father sounds like quite a philanthropist." Different from what she'd expected from a recluse monarch. "He sounds like you."

His hands stilled for the first time. "You're the first to say that."

"How would you describe your father?" She glanced back at him, catching a hint of tensed jaw before his face became a smooth, handsome mask again.

Carlos stared past her, through the portal, his massage resuming. "He's ill."

Not at all what she expected him to say. She tried to turn toward him but his touch became steely for the first time as he held her in place without hurting her, but unmistakably insistent.

Accepting his wishes to keep his face hidden from her, she gripped the window as clouds obscured the specks of light below. "I'm very sorry to hear that. What's wrong with him?"

"His liver is failing," he answered, his voice emotion-less other than a thickening of his accent. "During the escape from San Rinaldo, he spent a lot of time on the run in poor living conditions."

She'd read the basics about the coup in San Rinaldo, but there weren't many details available. Hearing the event from Carlos, envisioning the terror the Medinas—Carlos—must have experienced, made her chest go tight with pain for them.

"How awful that must have been for your family. I can't even begin to imagine."

"It was not an easy time in our lives," he understated simply. He stroked her shoulders, down her arms, never missing a beat even when his breathing became heavier against her hair. "We were not with him. My mother, my brothers and I went a different escape route once the rebels attacked. My father didn't want to risk us being captured with him so he attempted to make them follow him instead."

The picture unfolding in her mind was beyond imagining, but he seemed unwilling to take any comfort from her. Hell, he wouldn't even let her look at him.

"How old were you?"

"Thirteen," he answered starkly.

He traced up her arms again and stopped at the back of her dress. He slid a finger inside along her neck, just under the zipper, stroking one vertebra at a time. His sensuous touch was at such odds with their stark discussion, but then Carlos had always been a huge contradiction. The compassionate surgeon, gruff professional.

Tender lover, reserved friend.

And he clearly wanted to keep things on a physical level rather than emotional. How perfect since she'd thought the same thing herself not too long ago. Her head lolled forward and his hand tucked under the cashmere, fanning along either side of her spine, kneading nerve endings.

The zipper parted, only an inch, but still she gasped at the boldness of his move. Cool air brushed the tiny patch of bared flesh a second before his knuckles warmed her skin.

"Shhh," he coaxed. "I'm not doing anything other than rubbing your back to make the trip more comfortable."

She laughed softly. "Do you think I'm foolish?"

"Let me rephrase," he said against her ear. "I will not do anything more unless you ask."

Her heart stuttered at the image that conjured and the sensual power that gave her. What would it be like to claim the toe-curling bliss he could give her so easily?

So dispassionately?

She forced her thoughts to disengage from the path, dismayed to think he could pull away from her as smoothly as he could set her whole body to flame. No amount of temptation could lure her into that dangerous terrain. She wouldn't be his next Nancy Wolcott, sprinting to the shelter of her little hatchback car in the rain while Carlos watched with his cool, unmoved gaze.

"Well, take note then, Carlos, because I won't ask for more from you." She was only willing to let the physical side go so far. For now? Until when?

"That sounds like a challenge."

She turned slightly, meeting his eyes, their mouths so close every word was almost a kiss. "Do you really promise not to do anything more?"

With the full power of his intense dark gaze staring

at her with frank honesty and desire, there was no mistaking what he wanted. He wasn't thinking of any woman but her.

"You have my word. Tell me to stop and I will, without hesitation." His low, husky vow vibrated the air between them.

"Then by all means," she said, her voice breathier than she would have liked to admit, "continue what you were doing."

She could handle this.

Carefully, she turned her back to him again, her breasts prickling with awareness as she wondered how far this game between them would go. His hands spread and the zipper parted further link by link. The top of her dress stayed on even as cool recycled air swooshed over her back. He worked his way south to her waist, thumbs circling along small but persistent knots of tension and strain.

Down, down farther still, he went until massaging almost at the base of her spine, his skillful fingers teasing along the top of her bikini panties. His hands spanned all the way across her lower back, then wrapped forward to rub lightly against her hip bones.

Her dress eased precariously forward, until she crossed her arms to hold it in place. Yet she couldn't bring herself to tell him to stop. The pressure of his hands so intimately close to where she really wanted, *needed*, him to touch her only served to stoke the ache hotter.

They played with fire here and she knew it. Yet she trusted him when he said he wouldn't take this further without her permission. So she surrendered to the sensations washing over her.

The man had the art of touch mastered. The glide of his hands on her back soothed and stirred at the same time, the healer and the infuriating prince.

Oh God, it had been so long since she'd had a man's touch on her, his touch. Her body soaked up the gentle rasp of his callused fingers, his every move so precise as he explored her, relaxed her, totally in tune as to exactly where she needed his care.

According to the pregnancy books she'd read, the backaches would only grow worse, as if in some cosmic prelude to labor. Nerves pattered in her chest as her mind fast-forwarded, anxiety intensifying at the notion of facing that day alone.

"Shhh," Carlos whispered in her ear. His hands skimmed around to her rib cage and pulled her back against him. "Whatever you're thinking about. Don't. You're tensing up again. As much as I'm enjoying having my hands on you, I hate to think my efforts here have been for nothing."

His hands rested right below her breasts, so close her nipples peaked against her bra, tight and needy. As he stepped closer, his body against her back, the rigid length of him pressed to her spine with unmistakable arousal. She longed to writhe against him and tempt him higher, harder. How she burned to lift his palms to cover her breasts, to ease the ache with the warm pressure of him.

It was just physical, she reminded herself. Heaven knew she wasn't too happy with the man himself right now. But her willpower was beginning to wane.

She cuffed her fingers around his wrists and shifted his touch an inch lower. "I think it's time to call a halt to this."

Just that fast, his hands slid away. Not a word, not even a hint of a protest from him. However, her body shouted loud and clear over the loss of his touch. Her skin tightened, tingly and hot with awareness. Dragging in breaths that did nothing to steady her racing heart, she held her dress in place and faced him.

His features were taut, his eyes as molten as his dark cable sweater.

"We both—" Her voice shook and she steadied the betraying tremble before continuing, "We both know I'm attracted to you, and it's a safe bet to say you're attracted to me as well. I also know I can want you while not liking you very much. However, I'm not so sure that jumping each other is the wisest move—"

"Whoa, hold on there." He held up his hands while keeping them well off her. "I have no intention of seducing you."

"Oh." The guy sure knew how to take the wind out of a girl's sails. "Then what the hell was that erotic massage all about?"

He lowered his hands, still not so much as brushing her, while outlining her shape, her breasts, waist, hips, around and stopping an inch away from curving her bottom. "To put you at ease and reassure you of my self-control. You can enjoy what I'm about to do because you don't have to keep up your guard."

His confidence was unmistakable, the luxury cabin echoing with the regal sense of surety in his every word. Even in casual jeans and a sweater, this man was royal born, destined to lead, and right now she very much wanted to follow wherever he led.

A simple sway would bring her flush against him.

Breathe, she reminded herself. *Breathe.* "And what exactly are you about to do?"

He grinned ever so slightly at her words, his predatory look lifting the hairs on her arms.

"I'm going to kiss you."

Six

The luscious feel of Lilah still tattooed in his memory, burned in his brain, seared in his soul, Carlos lowered his mouth to hers. No subtle skim of lips over lips. He simply took her.

He'd warned her, giving her a chance to pull away. Still she had not uttered a syllable of protest, no request to stop. Perhaps that pushed the boundary of his promise to her, but he needed her to know how much he wanted her. It would hurt like hell to pull away, but he would honor his word.

He angled his mouth over hers more firmly, exploring, plundering, and wondered how she felt so familiar after only a few kisses. He would have recognized her taste, her scent, her fingers gliding along his jaw. Her touch was so exact, she could have been a surgeon herself, thoroughly dissecting his restraint and leaving him bare to the powerful draw of pure, undiluted Lilah.

She peeled away layers of his reserve as fully as she inched up his sweater and T-shirt to explore his chest with her cool, soft hands.

As smoothly as he'd eased the zipper down her dress earlier.

Sliding inside her open dress, he palmed her bottom. With only her silky panties between his fingers and her flesh, he fit her against him, his arousal. He'd told her they would use this time to find level ground but the floor beneath his feet felt more unsteady than ever.

She gripped fists full of his sweater, anchoring herself to him. So fast, so perfectly, she seduced him right back with a simple stroke of her hands, her tongue, her body brushing against his.

Already rock hard from wanting her, still he throbbed harder. Nobody turned him inside out the way Lilah did, until he forgot about the ever-present pain in his back, the persistent ghosts of his past. In her arms, he could even let go of his driving need to erase loss and agony from the endless stream of children who needed him, children who he too often failed….

And for all those reasons, he needed to keep himself carefully guarded around this woman. The one woman who could make him lose sight of his only path to redemption for his own failure.

Drawing in a shuddering breath that did little to sweep away the sense of Lilah invading every niche inside him, Carlos pulled away. Full of regret, he withdrew his hands and slipped her zipper up inch by inch until he cupped the back of her neck. He took in her passion-dazed emerald eyes, her kissed moist mouth, all signs of his effect on her.

She flattened her hands to his chest, her fingers plucking at his T-shirt peeking from the V-neck of his sweater. "I thought you weren't going to seduce me."

"You were seduced by just a kiss?" He took small comfort in that much.

"Don't be a jerk." Her smile went wobbly. "You know what you did."

"I also know what else I would like to do to you, but I promised not to take things further unless you asked." He tipped his ear toward the whine of jet engines. "Besides, I believe we are beginning our descent."

As if on cue, the intercom crackled a second ahead of the captain's voice. "This is your captain. Please return to your seats and buckle in for landing in Eagle-Vail, Colorado. On behalf of myself and my copilot, I hope you've had a pleasant flight."

They had arrived. And shortly, he would have Lilah all to himself in a house with eight empty bedrooms. He couldn't decide if he was a genius or a moron.

If there was even a remote chance that Lilah proved to be the mother of his child, they needed the chance to get to know each other better outside of the workplace. So this trip made sense. And the heat blasting over him even now from that kiss reminded him how good it could be between them.

But—baby or no baby—he needed to find a way to clear Lilah from his system before the need for her leveled all his defenses.

Permanently.

* * *

A few days alone in Vail, Colorado, with Carlos suddenly felt like an eternity.

As their SUV climbed the icy driveway winding up a hill, Lilah studied the house ahead of them and crossed her fingers for a large staff. Not because she wanted or expected to be waited on, rather she hoped for some human buffers between herself and the increasing need to jump the man beside her. She searched the looming structure for signs of life as Carlos spoke softly beside her, detailing enticing factoids about the area.

Of course he could make a hut in the woods sound amazing with that luscious accent.

The house, she reminded herself. *Check out the house.*

Three stories tall at the center, the cedar home sported varying heights and levels on either side in a sort of art deco Swiss Alps style that instantly charmed her. Built with logs that could only have come from the fattest, most ancient trees, the size of the structure seemed about right for the mammoth mountain it was perched on. Generous windows shone a welcoming yellow glow into the night, a positive sign there might be people inside.

Carlos guided the four-wheel drive past towering pines, branches still wearing heavy snowcaps. She hugged her coat tighter around her, which only served to remind her how much warmer his arms had been earlier in the airplane. Since the pilot had announced their approach, Carlos had shifted from seductive lover to considerate tour guide.

Finishing his spiel about amenities in Vail, he pulled the SUV into the six-car garage that appeared to be nearly two thousand square feet on its own. She'd grown up with affluence around her, but even she was taken aback a bit by the scope of vehicles surrounding her, everything from a Lamborghini to a Mercedes sedan to top-of-the-line snowmobiles.

Carlos might live a Spartan lifestyle in Tacoma, but apparently his family spared no expense when it came to their "toys."

Before she could unbuckle her seat belt, he'd come around to open her door, his shoulders broad in a black sweater and open ski jacket. His limp was more pronounced, reminding her what a long day this had to have been for him as well, yet he didn't complain. She'd noticed a cane in his office once, although she'd never seen him use it. He was a prideful man, no doubt. Offering him her arm would be out of the question.

What would it be like to have the freedom to slide her arm around his waist, intimately touching and helping without bruising his pride? No matter how well this time together went for them, she would never know that kind of closeness with Carlos. That stung her more than she could have foreseen a few short months ago.

Lilah followed him through the garage and into a narrow hall, pausing each time he stopped to disarm yet another security system, like peeling away layers of an onion. A very protected, paranoid onion. Hanging up her coat alongside his on a cast-iron coat tree, she eyed the massive floor-to-ceiling windows with new perception, suddenly certain the glass was bulletproof.

Trees had been thinned away from the house, giving a clear view of the empty snow-covered ground and walkways laid out with the precision of an English garden. Or a well-thought-out security plan...

Now *she* was becoming paranoid.

Focus on the perks of being here. Both indoor and outdoor pools loomed large, each with a breathtaking view of a distant snowcapped mountain range apparent even in the dark thanks to the last bit of twilight flaring along the peaks. She still hadn't seen any staff in the quiet house, only the sound of her footsteps and Carlos's on thick Aubusson rugs cutting the silence.

Walls were dotted with oil paintings of mountains, keeping with the chalet appeal. She had to admit it. He'd picked the perfect retreat.

"The Pyrenees," he filled in simply, referring to the range between Spain and France depicted in the paintings. "My family used to ski there."

Before the coup that destroyed San Rinaldo.

Before his birthright to be king had been stolen.

Before he lost his home, his mother.

She trailed her fingers along a carved mahogany frame. How many other hints of European heritage did he incorporate into his life that she must have missed over the years? How bittersweet those reminders must be of a home that had been ripped from him just as he stood on the brink of manhood.

He swept open the next door to an enormous gourmet kitchen, top-of-the-line appliances with stone and stainless steel decor. Dark green granite glowed under the heavy black iron pendant lamps illuminating the breakfast bar. A temperature-controlled wine refrigerator took up the entire base of a massive island, the exotic labels of the expensive vintages apparent through the lit glass doors.

Carlos leaned against the breakfast bar, feet crossed at the ankles. "The staff has been sent on vacation, but they left everything we should need to eat and a cleaning service will come in when needed."

Well, that answered the question about chaperones and buffers. She needed to put on her big girl hat and decide on her own whether or not she would sleep alone tonight. Or in his bed.

A whisper of longing huffed over her skin, and she loosened her hold on the coat she'd been clutching so tightly. Suddenly, she felt plenty warm. "I can wash my own dishes, thank you."

He pulled open the industrial-size refrigerator, dark blue denim hugging his hips. "Then what do you say to some food before we settle in for the night?"

Fifteen minutes later, she was curled up in the corner of an overstuffed sofa with Carlos sprawled on the couch across from her in the main living room. A roaring blaze crackled in the fireplace, warming her bare toes; her boots were resting beside the sofa. The polished stone hearth stretched up to the vaulted ceiling, the same as the stone fire pit outdoors on the sprawling rustic veranda that overlooked the mountain view. The whole place smelled like pine and cedar, right down to the fragrant wood crackling in the fireplace.

Still edgy from the kiss on the plane and woefully in need of something to ease the tension crackling through her veins, she cupped her mug of warmed cider, a plate of assorted finger foods on the end table beside her. Carlos devoured a larger, more substantial sandwich on pumpernickel. Not that he seemed to even notice how someone had gone to a lot of trouble to make even deli food look like a masterful creation, all the way down to the lettuce curling artfully around the edges.

He ate as he always did, efficiently, regarding the

food as nothing more than fuel for his body. The meal was nothing more than a necessary regimen, much like how he must wash his hands before surgery. She couldn't help but admire him in this moment. He had all of this wealth and privilege at his fingertips, yet he chose to live out his life serving others. There was an unmistakable honor in that.

Although she'd also seen in her job how easy it was for the driven humanitarians to burn themselves out. Perhaps he needed this time away for reasons he hadn't even begun to recognize.

Lilah sipped her cider, the stoneware warming her hands. "This place is…beyond words."

And it was exactly what she needed after the way work had overwhelmed her these last few months. The stress of finding out about the baby and not being able to share it with Carlos had taken its toll in ways she was only starting to appreciate. Right now, she couldn't help but feel grateful for this time out from real life to sort out her future. Somehow the secluded mountain mansion felt warm and welcoming. A safe haven in a crazy time.

At least she hoped it was the house making her feel that way and not the magnetism of the man.

Wiping his mouth with a linen napkin, he finished chewing. "Once my father accepted that his sons were not going to live their adult lives in hiding with him on his island, he tried to make sure our other properties were set up to have everything at our fingertips." Mug in hand, he gestured round the room with a semicircle sweep. "Less reason to step out into everyday society."

She shivered to think of all the worries a parent carried around in a normal world—to shoulder all the fears for his sons' safety that Enrique Medina faced seemed overwhelming.

Her hand slid protectively over her stomach. "He had reason to be fearful for your safety."

"Understood. But a life in hiding is no life at all." He polished off the last corner of his sandwich.

"Even if that life is spent in pampered luxury," she said, trying to inject a tone of levity into a suddenly too dark conversation.

"Especially so." He tossed his napkin on his empty stoneware plate and swung his legs up onto the sofa, almost managing to disguise his wince of discomfort. "All that said, however, this does make for one helluva vacation. It's even equipped with a golf room with a full swing simulator. Although we'll have to bypass the wine cellar this time since you're expecting."

This time? There would be more visits here?

Of course, once he realized this was his child there would be so many reasons for their paths to intersect. Whether or not he appreciated it yet, she knew her life was unequivocally intertwined with his forever. So many new concerns had come her way of late, it seemed impossible to absorb them all before another came rocketing through her brain. She struggled to follow his words.

He scratched the back of his neck, stretching the sweater taut across his broad shoulders. "The personal sauna is probably a no go too. I seem to recall from med school that pregnant women should use caution when it comes to saunas and hot tubs."

Heat flooded her face as she thought of their encounter in the hot tub at his place, the night they'd made the baby. His home had been starkly utilitarian except for the mammoth jetted bath, large enough for two. Intellectually, she knew he likely had the luxury installed for practical purposes because of his back, but they'd most certainly put the spa bathroom to totally impractical, indulgent good use that night.

The air between them snapped with awareness as she saw in his heavy-lidded eyes that he was remembering that night as well. And it affected him. Not surprising given their out-of-control kiss earlier on the plane.

But since that evening at the party when he'd really touched her for the first time, she hadn't been able to think of much else except the feel of his hands on her skin….

From the hospital rooftop garden, Lilah stared out at the Christmas lights twinkling through Tacoma's skyline. So intent on taking a breather from the overloud band and press of patrons at the party inside, she almost missed the sound of footsteps approaching behind her.

She stiffened in alarm, then heard the uneven gait she recognized well after four years of working with Carlos. And quite honestly, she could use the distraction of his company tonight after the disturbing call with her mother, in tears over finding the receipt for a nightie— red and not her size. Lilah gripped the icy rail tighter.

A second later, Carlos's hand skimmed her bare arms as he eased a velvet wrap around her shoulders. "Wouldn't want you to catch a cold out here."

"Thank you." She hugged her wrap closer as snow sprinkled from the sky. "You were especially nice to the board of directors tonight. I'm not going to grouse if you want to cut out early."

He stuffed his hands in his tuxedo pockets, dark eyes reflecting the string of tiny white lights strung around a potted evergreen. "Are you insinuating I've been less than polite in the past?"

"I know these sorts of gatherings aren't your thing." She scrunched her icy toes inside her pumps. "You usually have that vaguely tolerant look that lets us all know you've got one eye on your watch so you can get back to work."

"It's impossible to look at any watch when there's someone as beautiful as you to admire instead."

Her jaw dropped then snapped shut quickly. They'd been work friends for a long time, always careful never to cross that line. She'd accepted her attraction to him but never guessed he'd noticed her. "Uh, thank you?"

Her heart fluttered in a way that was totally out of character for her. She was usually so controlled.

"Obviously, I'm much better at hiding my emotions than you give me credit for if you've never noticed how you affect me."

A suspicion tugged at her mind. "Have you been drinking?"

"Not a drop." He crossed his heart with two fingers like the Boy Scout she couldn't picture him being.

"Me neither." Her breathy answer puffed into the cool night air.

"Actually, I've had a helluva day and something in your face tells me you have, too. The kind of day no alcohol can fix." He zeroed in with a perception that had her eyes stinging.

Thank goodness the rest of the partiers were still inside and out of sight. How he'd found her here, she didn't know. Maybe he needed the peace as much as she did.

She blinked hard and tried to tell herself it was just the biting wind making her tear up. Emotions aswirl like the spiraling snow, she boldly tugged both sides of his tuxedo tie. "You look quite stunning yourself, Dr. Medina."

His fingers banded around her wrists, hot and strong and so very enticing. Like him. "Then since we're both clearheaded, lovely Lilah," he whispered, nipping her ear once, lighting a static spark in her veins, "there's no reason not to do this."

Was that moan from her?

Deliberately, slowly, his lips grazed her cheek in a slow trek that had her gripping the rail to keep her legs from folding.

"And do this." His arms swept around her as he captured her next sigh with his mouth….

"Lilah?"

Carlos's voice startled her from her daze, back to the present in his Vail, Colorado, mountain retreat. The memory of his kiss then was as real and stirring as the one he'd given her earlier. She reached for her mug of cider, needing to ground herself in the moment. "I'm sorry. What did you say?"

She eyed him over the top of her mug, inhaling steaming scents of cinnamon as a log shifted in the fireplace, launching a shower of sparks. Those pinpricks of light didn't come close to the kind of sparks Carlos could set off inside her.

He set aside his mug on the coffee table. "Why have you never married?"

His abrupt shift to the personal stunned her into silence for two pops of the logs in the fireplace. How in the world had their conversation shifted to that topic while she'd been daydreaming? Not that she intended to offer up what she'd really been thinking about.

"Why haven't you?" she retorted carefully. "You're older than I am."

"Touché." He saluted her lightly. "I apologize for the sexist sound to my question. To show my contrition, I'll answer first. I decided a long time ago to stay a bachelor."

"Because…?" she asked, suddenly curious to the roots of her hair.

"Standard eternal bachelor reasons," he answered with a wry grin. "I'm a workaholic. I didn't want to subject any woman to the Medina madness."

The last reason was far from standard. "There have been women lining up outside your office ready to volunteer for that mayhem. In fact, Nancy seems ready to hustle to the front of the queue."

His smile flattened to a humorless scowl. "I haven't asked for or encouraged any of them."

"Yet still they flock to your side." The second the words left her mouth, she winced at sounding jealous. But she was carrying the man's child after all. Any of those women would be a part of her child's life through him.

Great. Now she was jealous *and* concerned.

Carlos massaged his knee absently. "They're flocking to the title and the money that comes with it. They wouldn't care if I was a troll with an extra eye in the middle of my forehead."

Laughter burst free and she clapped her hand over her mouth.

He cocked an eyebrow. "I wasn't joking."

"I know, but still, the image you painted…" She couldn't stop laughing. She knew the giggles had more to do with releasing tension than anything else. Her body was wound so tight from the events of the past two days she needed the outlet, a release for her swelling emotions.

And her emotions weren't the only thing that would be swelling soon. Her hand slid to her stomach.

Just the thought of that jolted a fresh burst of laughter until she clapped a hand over her mouth again. Carlos stared at her as if she was half-crazy, and maybe right now… Who knew? She hiccupped and a tear fell free. Then another. More. Until she couldn't stop the flood of an altogether different emotion as a sob tore its way through her heart and up her throat.

Seven

Carlos had seen patients cry more times than he cared to remember. Although he didn't like to think he'd become jaded, he couldn't afford to let tears sway him or he wouldn't be able to treat his patients.

But seeing Lilah so upset sliced through what little restraint he had left.

Unable to keep his distance, he swung his feet from the sofa and knelt beside her before she finished scrubbing her wrist across her cheeks. Only once had he known Lilah to lose it, about three years after he'd begun working for the Tacoma facility. She had gone to the mat with the insurance company for a patient of his, a child whose spine had been fractured in an amusement park ride accident—at the C7 vertebrae. The parents were supposed to be grateful their child could use his thumb to work the electric wheelchair.

Lilah had crushed opponents standing in the way of getting that boy everything he needed.

Late on the night of the boy's surgery, Carlos had been making rounds and found Lilah sitting by the kid's bed, a tear-soaked tissue in her hand. To this day he could envision her face in silhouette, a single tear clinging to her chin, as if that drop of water was every bit as stubborn as the woman, refusing to surrender. He'd never known why that case hit her harder than others, or if he'd just never before caught her during the emotional fallout. But something had shifted inside him then, releasing a gnawing need that dogged him until he gave in to temptation the night of the Christmas party.

A log dropped and popped as he knelt in front of her.

He knuckled a fresh tear from her cheek. "Are you all right?"

"Yes and no and I don't know." Her words jumbled on top of each other. "I almost wish I could blame it on hormones."

"The past couple of days have been overwhelming." For him, too.

"An understatement." She nodded tightly, her last bit of control obviously brittle.

Hooking his arm around her shoulders, he slid up beside her on the couch and drew her to his chest. Her shoulders trembled as she choked back sobs, then finally let go, crying into his sweater. He rested his cheek against the top of her head and inhaled the scent of her shampoo, lightly floral and so different from the antiseptic world they usually inhabited together. His hands skimmed up and down her spine, the soft cashmere reminding him of the massage he'd given her on the plane. Right now, though, her zipper would stay firmly in place. She needed something different from him and, by God, he would deliver.

He stroked her back, made what he hoped were soothing noises and held her until her tears slowed. Each gentle breath pressed her breasts to him. He gritted his teeth against the temptation to pull her closer and savor the lush curves of her. Nearly three months of no sex—of no Lilah—sent desire grating through him.

He felt like a bastard for being turned on while she was so blatantly upset. Protectiveness and passion got tangled up inside him. All the barriers he'd worked to resurrect around her crumbled.

Sniffling, she finally eased away, swiping her hair from her face and straightening her dress. She braced her shoulders and faced him, chin jutting with determination.

"Okay," she said simply.

Huh? "Okay what?"

"Let's make the most of this time away and have sex 24/7." She reached behind her neck to tug down the zipper on her cashmere dress. "Starting now."

Shock stunned him still until the rasp of her zipper brought him out of his stupor. Yes, he'd wanted her naked, but not this way, not when she wasn't thinking clearly.

Not when his own mind was such a mess.

"Whoa." He gripped her shoulders to keep the top in place, confused as to what brought her abrupt about-face and concerned about what had upset her. "Hold on there a second, Gypsy Rose Lee."

Her forehead pleated in frustration. "You're telling *me* to stop?"

GET 2 BOOKS

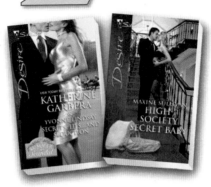

We'd like to send you two *Silhouette Desire*® novels absolutely free.
Accepting them puts you under no obligation to purchase any more books.

HOW TO GET YOUR
2 FREE BOOKS AND 2 FREE GIFTS

1. Return the reply card today, and we'll send you two *Silhouette Desire* novels, absolutely free! We'll even pay the postage!

2. Accepting free books places you under no obligation to buy anything, ever. Whatever you decide, the free books and gifts are yours to keep, free!

3. We hope that after receiving your free books you'll want to remain a subscriber, but the choice is yours—to continue or cancel, any time at all!

EXTRA BONUS

You'll also get two free mystery gifts! (worth about $10)

FREE!

BUSINESS REPLY MAIL
FIRST-CLASS MAIL   PERMIT NO. 717   BUFFALO, NY

POSTAGE WILL BE PAID BY ADDRESSEE

THE READER SERVICE
PO BOX 1867
BUFFALO NY 14240-9952

NO POSTAGE
NECESSARY
IF MAILED
IN THE
UNITED STATES

If offer card is missing, write to The Reader Service, P.O. Box 1867, Buffalo, NY 14240-1867 or visit www.ReaderService.com

"As much as it pains me to say this…" He took in the generous swell of her breasts so close, only an inch away from where he clasped her wrists. But he had to hold strong. "We need to talk this through."

Confusion faded from her face, replaced by increasing anger snapping from her as tangibly as the crackles in the stone hearth. "I'm not sure what kind of head game you're playing here, but I do not appreciate it. I could have sworn back in the plane today that you were totally turned on."

"Believe me, I was." He winced. "I am."

A slow, sexy smile creasing her face, she swayed closer, her green eyes glinting jewel tones. "Then what's stopping you?"

As much as it pained him, he forced out the words that would push her away for the night. "It would be wrong to take advantage of a woman when she's drunk or crying."

When they went to bed together again—and he was damn determined that they would—he wanted her every bit as certain as he was. Although the anger tightening her face made it clear his road back into her arms might not be smooth. He'd wounded her pride.

"Fine, then." She yanked up her zipper and swiped her fingers under her eyes a final time, clearing away all signs of tears.

Except for a tiny smudge of mascara streaking into her hairline. He thumbed the splotch and she jerked away.

He wished life's messes were as easily cleared. "Sleep on it. If in the morning when you're dry-eyed and rested you're still interested, then believe me, I'll have you on the nearest flat surface before the crepes cool."

The anger in her face eased a hint to reservation. "You can cook crepes?"

"Is that such a surprise?" He wanted to coax a smile to her face, end this day on a lighter note, anything to keep tears from her eyes. "I would have made them for you that morning if you'd stayed around."

She studied him with a narrowed, discerning gaze. "Is that what the cold shoulder has been about these past months? Because I left before breakfast? I remember things differently."

"Tell me what you recall." He could only think of how much he'd gone through the motions that morning, his insides shredded by the memories of his mother's assassination. He'd been intent on not letting Lilah get too close, maintaining the distance that protected him from a past he didn't stand a chance of reconciling.

"I remember the scent of bacon in the air along with the gruff tone in your voice and the way you hauled on your clothes for work." Hurt leaked into her voice, filling him with regret. "Can you deny that breakfast together would have been decidedly awkward?"

The last thing he wanted was to revisit the past in any form, especially given how poorly he'd handled it all in the ensuing months. He mentally kicked himself for bringing up that night in the first place. "Why don't we focus on now, rather than then? Meet me for crepes in about—" he glanced at his watch "—nine hours."

Steeling himself from taking things further tonight, he pressed a kiss to her cheek and tasted the salty remnants of her tears. He stood quickly before she could pull away or get angry again, and gestured the way toward her room. As she walked ahead silently, he realized that while her crying had stopped, he could still see the tension rippling through her spine. He'd accomplished nothing to help her.

God, he hated being mystified when it came to this woman. He always, always could reason his way through anything. But the way he felt about Lilah had wreaked havoc on his self-control.

With the scent of her still on his skin bringing back memories of their night together, it was all he could do to keep from charging after her and taking her up on her enticing offer....

He watched Lilah across the ballroom. Their kiss on the rooftop garden had spiraled out of control until they were seconds from having sex right there. Only the prospect of frostbite had convinced them to relocate. To his office. ASAP.

Anticipation ramped his heart rate as he tracked her making her way through the throng toward the exit, doing her best to disengage herself from the other partiers attempting to snag her attention. Jim—the head of pediatrics—was especially persistent, but then the guy wanted a substantial chunk of some grant money that had just come through.

Vaguely, Carlos registered his own name being called. He half glanced to find the new radiologist— Nancy Something—waving to snag his attention. He nodded politely then surged ahead before he could become entangled in a conversation. His full focus was on Lilah and their assignation.

His office was distant and private since Lilah had relocated his space after the Medina exposé hit the news and brought reporters rushing into his life. And speaking of the press, he checked his back to make sure no one followed him down the back hall.

He slid his key into the office lock just as a hand fell to rest on his shoulder. Lilah. Turning, he looped an arm around her and sealed his mouth to hers again, reaching behind to open the door.

Her fists tightened in his tux, her kiss increasingly frantic. Their legs tangling, he backed into his workspace, kicked the door closed and flattened her to the door.

He didn't know how this had flamed so high so fast, but he'd never wanted a woman as much as he had to have Lilah. Here. This minute.

Her hands fell to his pants and made fast work of his belt. Even now, the woman was bold and efficient. Strong. He admired that about her. He wanted to wrinkle her perfect dress, to ruck it up to her waist and bury himself inside her until she was lost in the moment. Out of control. Calling out his name. Especially with her fingers nudging down his zipper.

Good thing he was always prepared. He pulled the condom from his wallet and plucked out the packet of protection.

Reflexively, he pushed back thoughts of the children he would never have. Of how he didn't even dare risk adoption, risk exposing any child, any woman, to the dangers his family had faced. He would not, could not live through the nightmare of watching another woman suffer because of her connection to the Medina name.

Restraint shaky, he gathered Lilah's dress, bunching the silky fabric upward. He revealed his Grecian goddess inch by inch of creamy leg, nudged aside her panties and sunk inside. The warm clamp of her body

took him to a level beyond anything he'd experienced…
beyond anything he would feel again since this was the
only night he could have with her….

Embers blurring as he stared, Carlos rubbed his fingers together, the moisture from Lilah's tears soaking into his skin. Had he done the right thing in turning away from her, sending her to her room? Hell, half the time he didn't know what he was doing when it came to her. He reacted with his gut instead of his brain.

The tears she'd cried were so different from the ones shed by his patients and their worried parents. In those cases, he knew how to respond, his eyes firmly fixed on healing. Here, he didn't know how to ease her pain.

Then it hit him like the logs blazing back to life.

He was the cause of her tears and her tension. He'd sensed her anger the day she'd told him about the baby—tough to miss when she'd slapped him. But so intent on protecting her with distance, he'd missed the obvious.

Intellectually, he'd understood she believed him to be the father. He'd assumed she must have mixed up dates. Yet as he thought back to what she'd said in his office, he recalled her emphatic insistence that there hadn't been anyone other than him for months.

She had no reason to lie. Lilah had never been impressed by his money or his pedigree.

Bracing a steadying hand on the mantel, he let the implications line up in his brain. That left him with two possibilities. Either the baby really was his or someone had taken advantage of Lilah without her knowledge, not as far-fetched as it sounded. Some bastard could have slipped any number of date rape drugs into her drink. His hands fisted at even the possibility of her being taken advantage of so callously. So criminally.

A fresh wave of protectiveness—*possessiveness*—flooded him until he accepted the inevitable. She was his. Which made her baby his regardless.

The reality of that settled inside him. There was no cutting her out of his life. No turning his back. She and her child were his to keep safe. He hadn't planned on linking his life to anyone else's. Being a Medina had never brought peace to anyone, most certainly not to his mother.

But walking away from Lilah was no longer an option.

The next morning, Lilah combed her fingers through her damp hair, wide awake thanks to her shower. Sleep had been hard to come by.

Sure, she'd been reckless throwing herself at Carlos last night. Still, his rejection had hurt.

She hadn't cried again though. She'd refused to waste another tear on him. Instead, she'd stared dry-eyed at the soaring ceiling, warm honey-colored cedar planks overhead bathed in moonlight, then with the first morning rays.

Now the window let blazing sunshine through, but shed little illumination on her confused emotions. Hitching her jeans over her hips, she raised the zipper, then realized she couldn't button them any longer. Her waist was expanding. Time was ticking away to settle her life.

Could she trust he'd only pulled away out of honor? If so, could there be some hint to an answer about why he'd kept his distance in recent months?

Or was this just more of the same evasiveness from Carlos? There was only one way to find out.

Refusing to hide in her room all day, she yanked a pale pink angora sweater over her head—and down to cover her thickening waist. She would face whatever the day held with her eyes dry and her chin up. For her child. For her own pride. Lilah yanked open her bedroom door and padded down the hall, her socked feet sinking in the handwoven wool rugs. The second her foot hit the top step on the lengthy staircase, she smelled...

Breakfast. Sweet and fruity. Crepes, perhaps?

She'd almost forgotten about that part of their discussion, so focused on how he'd pushed her away. At the base of those stairs, a decision waited. Gripping the banister, she stared down and weighed her options, her heart racing. Her gaze settled on another of those framed oil paintings of the Pyrenees. She gripped the railing tighter, the reminder of Carlos's tumultuous childhood softening her heart just when she most wanted an excuse to be with him.

The sweet and bready scent of breakfast drifted up the stairs and this time she inhaled deeply, unreservedly soaking in this simple moment of domesticity from her royal lover. Each breath brought a surge of desire and anticipation as she thought of him preparing the meal for her, of him following through on his promise. He was showing her he hadn't been rejecting her last night—he'd truly been thinking of her.

Right now, she wanted him every bit as much as she had last night when she'd been so overwhelmed with fears about her future. Her hand settled on her stomach. The open button poked against her sweater, reminding her that all too soon she would need to put the concerns of her child first.

This could be her last chance to be with Carlos again.

Committed, she walked down the stairs and to the kitchen, the delicious aroma growing stronger. Her feet carried her closer, closer still, until she stopped in the cedar archway leading into the gourmet kitchen.

Carlos stood with his back to her, shuffling crepes from the stove to a serving platter. Plump raspberries and apricots filled a bowl. Her mouth watered, but more because of the broad shoulders of her personal chef than from the food itself. Her eyes lingered on his hands, as careful with the cuts on the apricots as he would be in the O.R. Strong, capable hands.

A copper tea kettle whistled and she nearly jumped out of her skin.

Pouring the water over a tea leaf infuser, he glanced back at her.

Lilah spread her hands wide. "No tears."

If he showed the least hesitation, she was out of here. She wanted him, but she'd made as much of a first step as her pride would allow.

He set aside a crystal flagon of syrup on the cutting board. His eyes flared with unmistakable heat. Her breath hitched at the power of his smile. Still, she didn't move, needing him to come to her.

One step at a time, he advanced, his limp reminding her of all the baggage they both brought to this encounter. Two wary people past the days of first-blush love.

Two people who couldn't deny the flame between them.

Carlos stopped in front of her in jeans and a plain

white T-shirt, his bare feet brushing her toes. "Are you hungry?"

"Starving," she answered, knowing full well neither of them referred to food. "No more talking."

No more chances for doubts and reservations to steal this moment.

He nodded. She exhaled a breath she hadn't even realized she'd been holding.

His hands slid up to span her waist with a bold large grip. She cupped his shoulder, ready, eager to step into his embrace.

In one smooth move, he lifted her onto the granite counter. She gasped in surprise. The stone chilled through the denim of her jeans. "Wow, somebody's in a hurry. Didn't anyone ever tell you not to bolt your food?"

"Apparently nobody's ever had anything as delectable as you on the menu."

He tore off a corner of the crepe and stirred it through the fruit. He brought the bite to her mouth. She tasted from his fingers. Her eyes slid closed at the burst of sensation on her tongue. The sweet fruit mixed with the lightly salty taste of his skin as he withdrew his fingers slowly. She couldn't resist sucking gently. His pupils widened in response. A low growl rumbled up his throat.

Pushing away the plate of crepes, she cupped the back of his neck, urging him closer. *Closer.* Until he stepped between her knees and kissed her. She tasted raspberries and syrup on his tongue. Apparently he'd sampled his own cooking along the way.

Her senses sharpened, the taste of him on her tongue, the scrape of his unshaven face under her fingers. The scent of fresh-washed man and the food he'd prepared for her filled her as tangibly as he would soon fill her body.

Clamping her legs around his waist, she locked him nearer, gripped by the connection she'd been aching to recapture. She banned all other thoughts from her mind but the here and now.

His hand slid under the hem of her sweater, his touch fiery against her bare flesh. He tunneled further until sweeping the angora up and over her head. He growled low in appreciation as he cupped her breasts. The creamy lace provided a flimsy barrier between her and his circling thumbs. Her nipples went hard, the lace suddenly itchy, her skin everywhere tightening with a need for more of his touch, more of him.

Arching toward him, she pressed for a fuller connection and he took her cue well. His hands slid behind her and freed her bra in a deft sweep.

She bunched his T-shirt, gathering, raising until she flung the body-warmed cotton across the room to rest on top of her sweater. She made fast work of the top button and zipper on his jeans while he tugged hers down her hips, lifting her briefly, then pulled them down her legs. He backed away, removing her pants inch by torturous inch.

His washboard stomach gleamed in the morning sun as she looked her fill at the strong expanse of his chest. She reached to trace down, down, down further still, following the crisp sprinkling of hair in a narrowing trail to his open button, down the links of his open zipper.

No underwear.

Carlos flung her pants to the floor and stepped closer.

The granite felt cool and slick against the backs of her bare legs. Only her silky panties separated her from total exposure. Her eager hand freed his arousal and his eyes slid closed. He flattened a palm on the counter for a second as if to steady himself.

A surge of feminine power curled through her as she stroked him, her thumb rolling over the glistening first pearly dampening. His throat worked in a long swallow before he opened his eyes. The intensity, the raw passion in his gaze left her breathless.

With slow deliberation, he swiped two fingers through the raspberries, squeezed the juice along her collarbone and cleaned it away with his mouth. The warmth of his tasting tongue and the cool air provided the most delicious contrast on her oversensitized skin. He nipped the last taste up at the base of her neck, then scooped up more of the fruit, eyeing her chest with only a hint of warning that he intended to...

Yes.

The drizzle of warmed juice flowed over her like the desire spreading throughout her body. Her head fell back as he laved his undivided attention on one breast and then the other. The gentle sucking along her skin and the light rasp of his tongue sent shivers of pure pleasure down her spine. She gripped his shoulders, her fingernails sinking in deep. He braced a hand against the counter and leaned into her.

A fleeting thought chased through her mind, concern for his back, for the strain he thoughtlessly put on his body. "Carlos, let's take this to the sofa."

Her fingers trailed down the flex of muscles on his back until she reached the puckered ridges of his healed flesh.

He popped a raspberry into her mouth. "I dreamed all night long about having you here." Pulling her hands away and replacing them on his shoulders, he nipped up her shoulder to draw on her bottom lip. "Nothing's going to steal that fantasy from me."

His words sent a thrill up her spine, almost chasing away her concern for him. She sought a way to express her worry without stinging his pride. "But what if…"

"What if my legs give way?" He raised an eyebrow and hooked a finger on either side of her skimpy panties. "Then you can join me on the floor and we'll finish there, because don't doubt for a minute we're taking this to the conclusion we both want."

He twisted his fingers in the fragile fabric until her panties gave way. "I will see this through any and every way I can have you."

Air brushed along her damp and needy core, stirring her higher. Just air, for heaven's sake. Her heart tripped over itself in anticipation of his touch.

He inched her hips nearer to the edge. "Condoms or no condoms? I'm clean. There's been nobody but you in a year."

A year? His words along with the thick pressure of him, right there so close, teased her perilously near completion too fast.

"Go ahead," he urged, "let go. I'll take you there again as many times as you want."

His bold confidence sent a charge through her, reminding her of how he'd coaxed her to let go before. And she realized—he wasn't going to fall. He was in complete control of this moment between them.

"There is no need for a condom, Carlos. None. It's only you and me."

Her fingers dug deeper into his flanks as he thrust inside, his low growl of possession echoing through the spacious kitchen. Clamping her legs around his waist again, she urged him deeper, faster. Still she wanted more of him, no restraint. She whispered her wishes, her wants, her secret fantasies in his ear, delighting in the feel of his throbbing response to her words.

Just like after that party, she lost herself in the frenzy of the moment. Even wondering all night long if this would happen, still the powerful need caught her unaware. She'd known their sex was one of a kind before, but her memories…well… Nothing could compare to the pulsing draw she felt now in his arms.

Carlos brought her just shy of release again and again until their bodies were slicked with sweat. The scent of them together blended with the sweet stickiness of the raspberries and sugary fruit juice.

Flattening her hands behind her on the counter, inching closer, closer again, hungry to be nearer still, she rolled her hips against his. Her eyes fluttered open and shut, giving her glimpses of the mountain range stretching across the horizon. They were completely isolated up here, alone to explore each other, to explore the complex, confused feelings that had erupted between them over the past few months.

His pulse throbbed in his temple. He dipped his head to her breasts, increasing her pleasure with a flick of his tongue. The tingling in her veins gathered low and pulsing, tighter still until she gasped.

Once.

Twice.

The third carried her moan of release to echo into the cedar rafters. Sweet sensations exploded inside her, filling every corner until she could have sworn even the roots of her hair shimmered.

She bowed upward and into his arms as he thrust again, again, again, until finishing with a hoarse shout muffled against her neck. The throb of his completion triggered an aftershock through her. Caught unaware, she shuddered, her bare chest against his. Her arms went limp with exhaustion around his neck. She tried to hold on but her body had gone boneless with bliss.

Carlos's hold on her tightened just in time to keep her from slipping off the counter. "Lilah?"

"What?" she answered simply, unable to scrounge more than the single syllable.

His fingers dug deeper into her hips, giving only a second's forewarning of his increased intensity before he demanded, "Marry me."

Eight

The force of his release still pounding through his veins, Carlos wondered how he'd let amazing sex steal his ability to think rationally. He hadn't meant to blurt out his proposal quite that way. As he'd prepared breakfast, he'd planned for something more…eloquent maybe, after they shared crepes in front of the soaring mountain view.

Feeling Lilah frozen in his arms relayed her shock, but not much else. He searched her face for some hint as to how she felt, but she quickly averted her eyes.

Silently, Lilah inched to the side and back to the floor. She snatched his T-shirt from the butcher block and yanked the white cotton over her head in a swift move. With defiant eyes, she all but dared him to comment on the fact she wore his shirt.

Her bravado waning fast, her hands shook as she

pulled free her sex-tousled hair. "Um, we've already had sex, more than once I might add. So a proposal for 'compromising' me isn't in order."

"You didn't answer." He zipped and buttoned his jeans, wincing.

Fisting her hands by her side, she finally faced him full-on. "My answer is no."

Her refusal stung him more than he would have expected. He didn't want to get married, damn it. "I thought you would be happy. You didn't even think about my proposal."

"And you did?" she retorted.

He might be confused about a number of things when it came to this woman, but he could answer this question honestly. "It's all I thought about."

"Why did you ask me? And why now of all times?" She padded closer across the tile until she stood toe-to-toe with him. "Is it because I shed a few tears last night? Am I suddenly one of your needy cases to save?"

"I want the child to be mine." He gripped her shoulders, working to keep the fierceness inside him from escaping. "I want to protect you both. Is that so wrong?"

She shook her head fiercely. "That's not the same as believing me."

Why did she have to keep pushing this? He was doing what she must have wanted from the start. What he had to do now. "I'll take care of you and the baby, claim it as mine, regardless of what the test shows. You and I are alike. We make a logical match."

"A logical match," she repeated cynically. "Your single life suited you fine up to now. You've said so yourself on more occasions than I can count. In the four years we've known each other, you haven't even hinted—"

Frustration tore at his gut as he tried to find the right words to offer her. "What the hell do you think that night we spent together was about?"

"I don't know, Carlos." Her jaw went tight, but she didn't shed even one of the tears sheening in her eyes. "I do know that the months that followed were about you moving on as if I didn't exist. Maybe I'm not as logical or practical as you believe, because I couldn't just rationalize away the time we spent together."

He should have waited and proposed as he'd planned, in more of a romantic setting. He scrambled for something to say to give her more of the flowers and stars kind of affirmation he should have offered in the first place. "What we experienced rocked me."

"That's it? I rocked your world?" Shaking her head, she backed up. "Well, hello, you rocked my world, too. It's called great sex. Not something particularly logical to build a marriage on."

Spinning away, she made fast tracks toward the stairs, proving loud and clear how badly he'd messed up.

"Lilah! Lilah, damn it. Let's talk this out." He started after her.

His cell phone rang from beside the bowl full of raspberries and memories of tasting Lilah. He reached to thumb the ignore button, only to hesitate when he saw his youngest brother's number on the caller ID. He had to take the call. Maybe giving Lilah a few minutes to cool down would be a wise idea anyway.

"Antonio?" he said into his phone. "Speak to me and it better be important."

"It is." His brother's voice filled the airwaves. "It's

our father. He's taken a turn for the worse. The doctors don't expect him to live through the week if he doesn't get a liver transplant."

Leaving Vail far behind, Lilah peered through the airplane window at the dark sky and clouds. From her work at the hospital, she'd seen often enough how a family health crisis derailed any other concerns.

Just when she'd thought her life couldn't be flipped upside down any further.

Once she'd returned to the kitchen in her clothes, she'd been ready to roll out a speech she prepared, asking him to stop any further marriage proposals or she would leave. The news about his father had changed everything. Carlos had asked her to come with him. How could she say no?

This could be her only chance to meet her child's grandfather. She could learn important information about Carlos that might help her deal with him in the future.

And there was one completely illogical, emotional reason to stay right by his side. She couldn't let him face his father's death alone, especially not when he'd asked for her. Carlos never asked for anything for himself. Ever.

So here she sat, on the plane with him again. This time they were flying through the night sky to some super-secure island off the coast of Florida, which was more information than she'd ever read in the media about the location of his well-protected father. That Carlos would tell her such a closely guarded secret stirred a scary kind of hope inside her. In spite of his unromantic proposal chock-full of "practical" and "logical" reasons to get married, they obviously still shared a respect and trust that they'd possessed once upon a time as friends.

Well, at least as far as either of them seemed capable of trusting, which wasn't saying much.

Sitting across from her as before, Carlos checked his messages, his face inscrutable. The window beside him displayed the receding U.S. shore as they traveled over a murky view of ocean waters.

Their packing and leaving had been so rushed she'd barely had a chance to process their explosive encounter in the kitchen. The scent of raspberries still clung to her skin even after her hurried shower.

The casual lover was long gone now, replaced by the preoccupied doctor she knew so much better. His gray suit was tailor-made, fine quality, yet it hung a bit loose on his lean muscled body, as if he worked so hard he forgot to eat—or get a haircut. She clenched the armrests to resist the temptation to stroke back the salt-and-pepper hair brushing his brow.

With a muttered curse, he jammed his phone inside his jacket again.

She toyed with a loose string along the hem of her dress, her clothing options becoming limited until she went shopping for maternity jeans. "Anything new about your father's condition?"

Shifting uncomfortably in his leather seat, he shook his head. "Only a message from my youngest brother confirming our arrival time."

"I'm sorry. You must be frantic."

He stared at his hands clasped loosely between his knees. "It's not like I haven't known this day was coming soon."

"We've both seen enough cases at the hospital to realize that preparation doesn't erase the pain."

"Talking about it won't change anything." He waved away her sympathy and straightened abruptly. "I apologize for springing the whole family on you so abruptly. I had planned to hold off on that until the end of our time alone."

Surprise cut through her. He'd never mentioned planning this trip to meet his relatives. More of those confused and warily hopeful feelings stirred in her gut. "Both of your brothers are already there?"

"My brother Antonio, his wife and stepson. Duarte and his fiancée. And my half sister is there with her husband. I'm surprised she traveled so late in her pregnancy, but Antonio said she's emphatic about being there." He pinched the bridge of his nose as if battling a headache. "Sorry to introduce so many people at once. The estate is large enough for you to have your own space if you need to escape. My brothers and I each have our own wing. There's also a guesthouse if you prefer that to staying with me. "

"I'm sure your wing will be fine."

"The island is secure, without question, but there's everything you could need there. Our father built it all—from a clinic to a chapel to an ice cream parlor café. He said he wanted us to have 'normal' childhood memories, whatever those are."

"It sounds like your father tried to do his best in an unimaginable situation."

"The violence directed at our family was very real and damn dangerous." He extended his legs in front of him, drawing her attention to the way his muscular thighs stretched the fine gabardine, the sinews defined so well that the veneer of luxury didn't begin to mask the raw power of the man underneath the clothes. "Actually, I appreciated the privacy when I lived there. My brothers hated it on the island, but I didn't want any part of the real world again."

Why had he left if he felt that way? Then she realized. "Now I understand how you work those insane hours at the hospital. You actually don't mind being cut off from day-to-day life."

Carlos arched an eyebrow, half smiling. "Is that a loaded question to figure out if I can change enough where you could envision living with me?"

Admiration and attraction weren't going to be enough to make a relationship work. "You're assuming I'm willing to live with you."

All humor faded from his face. "I want us to do more than live together. I meant what I said back in the kitchen. I want us to be married."

Married?

The word still packed a powerful jolt. She knew part of her knee-jerk reaction to the idea had to do with the train wreck that was her parents' screwed up union. But she knew this would be rushing it.

As much as she didn't want to upset him when he had such heavy worries about his father, she couldn't let this marriage nonsense continue. What if he said something in front of his family? "If you keep proposing, I'll have to sleep in that guesthouse. This was about no pressure, remember?"

"Then let's back up to the living together." His eyes narrowed with that sleepy-sexy look she was beginning to recognize so well. "More importantly, let's get back to *not sleeping* together."

His words stirred memories of frantic lovemaking on the counter, bringing the sweet taste of raspberries exploding through her senses like the aftershocks of a world-rocking orgasm. She suspected he wasn't really serious, but rather found such outrageous talk a distraction from concerns about his father.

All the same, she squirmed uncomfortably in her seat, leather creaking as the tension and the need inside her increased. "Now that you've mentioned sleeping, I think I'll catch a catnap for the rest of the flight."

"Fine," he said, a wicked gleam mingling with the steam in his eyes. "But remember that bacon cheeseburger and mint milkshake you said you'd been craving? The steward has both ready for you. Of course, I can cancel the order."

Her mouth watered. And quite frankly, she welcomed the lighter air he seemed determined to inject. Weightier concerns would come soon enough once they landed. "You're using food to blackmail an expectant mother into conversation? That's not playing fair."

"I'm only trying to help," he said practically. "I want to take care of you. Not just what you eat or helping you with an aching back. Getting married makes sense."

Deftly, he'd shifted the conversation right back to that confusing proposal of his. What was his real motive for this about face?

Yet what did *she* want? Her heart clenched as she realized she was more like her mother than she cared to admit, because she did want the fairy-tale romanticism after all. "Thank you, but in case you haven't noticed, I'm capable of taking care of myself."

Silence stretched between them until she looked away, focusing instead on the view below where Carlos's family waited. And what about *her* family? She couldn't delay calling them for much longer. She just wanted to have her life more settled first.

She wanted to have her feelings for Carlos resolved.

In the distance, an island rested in the middle of the murky ocean. Palm trees spiked from the landscape, lushly thick and so very different from the leafless snowy winter they'd left behind.

Curiosity about Carlos's home drew her until she nearly had her nose pressed to the glass as she catalogued details. It was a small city unto itself, a surprise splash of lights in the sea so vast that, like a Lite-Brite design on the water, the island began to take shape. A dozen or so small outbuildings dotted a semicircle around a larger structure, what appeared to be the main house, bathed in floodlights.

The white mansion faced the ocean in a U shape, constructed around a large courtyard with a pool. Details were spotty in the dark. Soon enough she would get an up close view of the place where Enrique Medina had lived in seclusion for over twenty-five years, a gilded cage for his sons to say the least. Even from a distance she couldn't miss the grand scale of the sprawling estate.

The intercom system crackled a second before the pilot announced, "We're about to begin descending to our destination. Please return to your seats and secure your lap belts. Thank you, and we hope you had a pleasant flight."

Her stomach knotted with nerves over meeting his family.

Engines whining louder, the plane banked, lining up

with a thin islet alongside the larger island. A single strip of concrete marked the private runway, blinking with landing lights in the night. As they neared, a ferryboat came into focus. To ride from the airport to the main island? They sure were serious about security.

She thought of his father, a man who'd been overthrown in a violent coup. The detailed planning of the island made her wonder if every step this family made had ulterior motives. Nothing seemed left to chance.

If that was the case, why then had he brought her here?

Carlos steered the SUV through the scroll-work gates separating his father's mansion from the island. The machine gun-toting guards didn't so much as flinch as he drove by. He and his siblings had agreed to gather at the house to reconnoiter, then go to the island clinic to see their father.

He thought he'd prepared himself for this visit, prepared himself for his father's death. But as he stared at the white adobe mansion where he'd spent his teenage years recovering, the past came roaring up like a rogue tidal wave.

Slowing the vehicle, he eased past a towering marble fountain with a "welcome" pineapple on top. Ironic.

When he'd been here for his brother's wedding, he'd been able to numb himself. However, for some reason, he felt raw this time in a way that he hadn't experienced since a surgeon had retooled most of his insides. His fingers clenched around the steering wheel reflexively before he forced himself to relax and turn the vehicle over to the uniformed staff member opening the passenger door.

His shirt stuck to his back, and Carlos tried to chalk up the perspiration to the warmer Florida climate. But he couldn't lie to himself. The doctor inside him couldn't deny the physiological reaction to the stress of being here.

Carlos circled the front of the car and before he consciously registered the motion, he reached for Lilah. Strange how her presence here kept him going. One foot in front of the other, in spite of the stabbing pain increasing at the base of his spine. His body shouted subliminal alarms left and right. He tucked his hand against her waist under the guise of being gentlemanly since she would probably think he was nuts if he clasped her hand.

This arrival together was important to him, a commitment from him to her, even if she didn't realize it. Bringing any outsider to the island was a huge step. Especially for him. His family would recognize that right away.

Lilah was his now.

The butler motioned them toward the library. Lilah stayed silent, eyeing her surroundings as they walked through the cavernous circular hall, two staircases stretching up either side, meeting in the middle. He guided her through the gold gilded archway, past his father's favorite Picasso.

Finally, he reached the library, his father's domain. Books filled three walls, interspersed with windows and a sliding brass ladder. Mosaic tiles swirled outward on the floor; the ceiling was filled with frescos of globes and conquistadors. Scents from the orange trees drifted in through the open windows along with the feel of the ever-present warm ocean breeze.

Beneath a wide skylight, the family had all gathered while his father's wingback chair loomed empty. Enrique's two Rhodesian ridgebacks stood guard on either side of the empty "throne."

"Lilah, these are my brothers, Duarte and Antonio."

Duarte stepped forward first, his hand extended precisely. His middle brother would have made the perfect military officer if they'd stayed in San Rinaldo. Their assumed identities as adults had made it impossible for Duarte to sign on as a U.S. serviceman. Instead, he'd become a ruthless businessman.

Lilah wore her overly calm expression, the one Carlos had seen her wear during stressful board meetings at the hospital. She shook Antonio's hand next.

The family maverick sported longer hair. He'd left the island at eighteen and signed on to a shrimp boat crew in Galveston Bay, working his way up to shipping magnate. His weathered face showed lines of worry today. His new wife tucked her arms around his waist in quiet comfort.

Once intros were complete, the women circled Lilah in an impenetrable wall—of protection or curiosity? He wasn't sure. But their half sister, Eloisa, Antonio's wife, Shannon, and Duarte's fiancée, Kate, were filling her ears with everything she could possibly need to know about the island.

Carlos turned to his brothers. "Our father?"

Duarte clasped his hands behind his back. "Still holding his own at the clinic."

"I want to know why he left the hospital in Jacksonville." There had been a glimmer of hope when they finally persuaded their father to look beyond the island clinic for medical help on the mainland. Getting their father to agree had been a major coup given what a recluse Enrique had become. "I thought he was on board with seeing specialists."

Antonio shrugged impatiently. "He said he's come home to die with his family."

Duarte's jaw went tight for a second before he continued, "The doctors in Jacksonville support the clinic staff here. Transplant is the only way to go if he wants a chance at beating this."

"Then what's with his whole death march?" Their father had options. A chance. A liver transplant could even be done with a live donor giving a lobe of his or her liver, and Enrique had a room full of possibilities in his children. "We need to get him back to Jacksonville immediately."

Duarte laughed darkly. "Good luck convincing him to agree."

Antonio braced a hand against the dormant fireplace. "Tests show I'm a match as a donor, but the old man shut me down. He's fixated on the notion that he doesn't want me to undergo the risk, even though it will save his life."

Carlos resisted the urge to bark out his frustration at the outright hypocrisy. His father had demanded his son fight to live after the bullets had torn into his back, to endure endless torturous procedures and rehabilitation in order to beat the odds and walk again. No way was Carlos letting the old man simply check out on the family when there was still a chance. "I will just have to persuade him otherwise."

"We would have called you about this sooner, but

you're ineligible to be a donor because of the damage to your liver from the gunshot wounds."

A gasp drew his attention. He turned to see Lilah staring back at him with wide—surprised—eyes, the color draining from her creamy skin. Hell. He'd never told her the real cause of his injuries and he hadn't thought to warn his brothers to stay silent on the subject.

It hadn't seemed necessary to inform her. There hadn't been the right moment. And he knew those were just excuses because he didn't want to revisit that time in his life with anyone.

Seeing the confusion in her eyes, he realized he'd screwed up with her yet again, and that unsettled him as he accepted just how important it had become to have her with him.

Talking with Lilah would have to wait, however. He needed to prepare himself to see his father for what could be the last time.

Nine

Every minute spent on this island only imprinted in her brain how very little she knew about the man who'd fathered her child.

High heels echoing down the marble corridor, Lilah trailed the other women as they gave her a crash course on the Medina mansion, a palatial retreat that felt nearly as large as the Tacoma hospital. They'd already seen the library, music room, movie screening room, pools, more than one dining area and her own suite. Now she was learning where to find the others in their quarters.

Too bad she couldn't just MapQuest the place.

Maybe as she wandered she could collect clues about Carlos from the priceless art collection on walls and pedestals.

Her heart clenched as she remembered the only painting on the wall in his hospital office—a canvas by Joaquín Sorolla y Bastida, one of the *Sad Inheritance* preparatory pieces. She'd always thought the image of crippled children bathing in healing waters to be tied into his own work.

Now she realized how he was connected to that image in a far more tragic way than she could have ever known. Shot in the back? Tears stung her eyes as she envisioned his scars with a deeper understanding.

So far the house wasn't revealing much more about him other than relaying an utter isolation and wealth beyond anything she could have imagined. Her only other option? Ask.

Passing yet another heavily armed and stoic guard, she eyed the women in front of her. Carlos's dark-haired sister Eloisa. Then the girl-next-door blonde sister-in-law, Shannon. And the savvy-eyed brunette fiancée, Kate.

The time with them would be better spent picking their minds about the family than memorizing the floor plan of this mansion maze. She just hoped they weren't as closemouthed as Carlos. Angling to the side, she passed a man vacuuming the molding over a high archway. Given the late hour, she wondered if the staff around here ever slept.

As they walked through a small courtyard, she ran her hand along a sleek jade cat keeping watch over a fountain nestled between the property's vast wings.

Shannon opened yet another door in their marathon tour. "This hall leads to my quarters." Her Texas twang coated each word as silk Italian drapes rippled with their passing. "I hope you won't mind if I check on my son real quick and relieve the nanny. Then we can have that late-night snack I promised."

"Please, take your time," Lilah said, waving the younger mother into the room, balcony doors already parted to admit a gusty ocean breeze. "I'm wide awake on West Coast time."

Soon she would have those same responsibilities, the privilege of a child in her life. Making sure her child had the most stable life possible increased the urgency in settling her confused feelings about the baby's father.

Her shoes sunk into the Persian rug until the toes blended into the apricot and gray pattern as she followed the other women into the rooms Shannon shared with Antonio. The suite sported two bedrooms off a sitting area with an eating space stocked more fully than most kitchens. Seeming to know her way around, Kate brought a tray with a bone china teapot alongside a plate of tiny sandwiches and fat strawberries.

Lilah lingered by a Waterford vase to sniff the lisianthus with blooms resembling blue roses that softened the gray tones in the decor. Trailing her fingers along the camelback sofa, she hesitated, surprised to find a homey knitted afghan.

Softly, Shannon closed her son's door and crossed to the sofa, caressing the worn-soft pewter yarn with reverence. "Their mother made this for Antonio shortly before she died." She looked up, her blue-gray eyes sad. "Antonio was only five when they left San Rinaldo. He told me he thought of the blanket as a shield."

Five years old.

As the other women settled into fat, comfy chairs, Lilah wrapped her arms around herself, chilled to the core by the image of three young boys fleeing the only home they'd ever known. Dodging bullets. Losing their mother. She squeezed her eyes shut briefly. In the four years she'd known Carlos, she hadn't a clue just how deep and dark those shadows in his eyes went.

Sweeping her sleek, black ponytail over her shoulder, Eloisa propped her feet on an ottoman, balancing a plate of shrimp and cucumber sandwiches on top of her pregnant belly with a wry grin. "It's more than a little overwhelming, isn't it? I'm still growing accustomed to all of it."

Resisting the urge to touch her own expanding waistline, Lilah focused on the woman's words instead, eager to learn more about these people who would be family to her baby. "Didn't Enrique have visitation rights when you were a child?"

"My parents never had an official custody agreement drawn up. I only met him once." Eloisa leaned forward for her tea, her silver shell charm necklace chiming against her china plate. "I was about seven at the time of my visit."

Taking a cup of tea from Shannon, Lilah reviewed what little she knew about the Medina history. "That's years after the last sighting of him."

Eloisa smiled nostalgically. "I didn't know where we went when my mother and I flew here. It felt like we took a long time in the air. But of course all travel seems to take forever at that age. I never told anyone about the visit after I left here. I may not have had much of a relationship with my father while I was growing up, but I understood that his safety and the safety of my brothers depended on my silence."

Shivering, Lilah eyed the blanket made by a mother who would never see her children grow up. "Did you meet them as well?"

She sipped her tea to warm herself in spite of the sultry

island air. A burst of chocolate mint flavor surprised her. Had Carlos informed the staff of her recent craving for chocolate mint? The possibility seeped through her more tangibly than the drink.

"Duarte and Antonio were here," Eloisa answered. "Carlos was having treatments at the time."

Her teacup rattled on the saucer. Lilah set it down carefully and busied her shaking hands by picking from the assortment of tiny round sandwiches—goat cheese and watercress. "The whole trip must have seemed strange to you, a child so young."

"More than you know." Eloisa smiled as Shannon held out a tray of fruit—she selected a chocolate strawberry with obvious anticipation. "My mother had remarried by then and had another baby."

Her words sunk in. "How did your stepfather feel about the trip?"

"He never knew about the visit, or about any of the Medinas...until recently when the whole world learned too."

Shannon settled back into her chair, tucking her bare feet under her, expensive shoes forgotten in the timeless ritual of girl talk. "The day that revelation exploded on the internet is definitely one of the most memorable moments of my life."

The everyday sort of gab session wrapped around Lilah with a strange—alien?—feeling. She had so few people in her life to share moments like this. As the only daughter with two much older brothers, as a woman with a high-powered position, she didn't have many female friends with whom she could kick off her shoes.

Lilah accepted a refill from Kate. "When our hospital staff first heard the news, the whole place went wild over the fact that one of our own surgeons had been leading a double life."

She couldn't imagine such an existence of secrecy and fear. She'd been so focused on Carlos's injuries that she hadn't considered how other aspects of his childhood had shaped him as well.

Eloisa waved a hand dismissively. "But my childhood, the whole exposé—" she winked at Kate, whose photos had first started that buzz "—it's all water under the bridge now. I want to tell you about that visit when I was seven. It was amazing, or rather it seemed that way to me through my childish, idealistic eyes. We all walked along the beach and collected shells. He—" she paused, clearing her throat "—um, Enrique, told me this story about a little squirrel that could travel wherever she wanted by scampering along the telephone lines."

Lilah reached to clasp the other woman's hand. "What a beautiful memory."

Would these two Medina grandchildren—Eloisa's baby and Lilah's child—have the privilege of hearing their grandfather Enrique tell them the same story?

Reconciling the image of a man who would tell such lovely tales with the notion of a father ignoring his child unsettled Lilah. Greatly. A man who could detach himself came into focus, bringing fears because Carlos had sliced her from his life just as easily.

Had he learned that skill at his father's knee? Could she be in for another repeat in the future, regardless of how open he'd seemed in the Colorado kitchen?

The attorney inside her blared warnings to protect herself, protect her baby against a family with unlimited resources at their fingertips. People with this kind of power rarely surrendered anything. Once Carlos had the proof in hand about the baby, she didn't doubt for a second that he would claim his child with a fierce determination.

Would he go so far as to try to gain custody of the baby if she didn't marry him? And could she put aside a lifetime of reservations about relationships to agree to a marriage of convenience?

No matter the warm draw of the women around her, the hope of a secure life for her, for her baby—for Carlos—provided a frighteningly heavy allure.

Carlos guided the four-wheel drive over the two-lane paved road, Duarte beside him and Antonio in the back. Only a couple more minutes until they reached the island clinic—and their dying father. He thought he'd prepared himself for this day.

But he was wrong.

Of course he'd been mistaken about a lot of things lately, like assuming Lilah would jump at the chance to marry him. The way she'd thrown his proposal back in his face still grated. As much as he tried to play things calm and laid-back with offers of cheeseburgers and milk shakes, he couldn't escape the sense that time was slipping away. That if he didn't settle his life soon, there wouldn't be another chance for him with her.

In the backseat, Antonio leaned forward, arms resting on the backs of his brothers' seats. "Care to share, Carlos?"

His hands tightened around the steering wheel as he steered deeper into the jungle. "About what?"

"Really, brother." Antonio flicked him on the temple. "You're supposed to be the genius in our family. Who's the lady friend?"

"Lilah and I work at the same hospital. She's the administrator."

"A lawyer?" Duarte loaded the final word with cynicism, his arm hooked out the open window.

Antonio snorted. "You're the one engaged to a *reporter*."

"Photojournalist," Duarte corrected softly, possessively.

Protectively.

His fiancée had been the one to first break the Medina story to the press with a picture she'd accidentally nabbed. Ironically, that snapshot had brought her and Duarte together and now she handled all carefully controlled press releases about the family.

Their youngest brother chuckled. "Journalist or photojournalist. Tomato, tom-ah-to."

Carlos whipped the car around a corner, toward a one-storey building, white stucco with a red tile roof. The clinic sported two wings, perched like a bird on the manicured lawn. One side held the offices for regular checkups, eye exams and dental visits. The other side was reserved for hospital beds, testing and surgeries. The clinic treated not only the Medinas, but also the staff needed to run a small island kingdom.

Everything was top-of-the-line, easy enough to finance with an unlimited bank balance. Enrique had insisted on the best for the facility where his son would spend most of his teenage years. Carlos knew every nook and cranny of the place.

"Ignore Antonio," Duarte said, bracing a hand on the dash. "I'm happy for you, my brother."

Downshifting as he cruised to a stop in front of the double sliding doors, Carlos glanced at his brothers quickly. "Hold off on the congratulations." Better to be honest than risk them congratulating Lilah. "I still have to convince her."

Carlos pocketed the keys and left the vehicle. Guards nodded a welcome without relaxing their stance. Electric doors slid open. A blast of cool, antiseptic air drifted out. The clinic was fully staffed with doctors and nurses, on hand to see to the health concerns of the small legion that ran Enrique's island home. Most were also from San Rinaldo or relatives of the refugees.

Antonio pointed to the correct room number, although Carlos would have known from the fresh pair of heavily armed sentinels. Enrique never relaxed security. Ever. Even when at death's door.

Duarte stopped Carlos with a hand to the arm. "We'll wait out here so you can have time to visit him on your own first. Call when you're ready for us to join you."

Carlos nodded his gratitude, words stuck in his throat underneath the wad of emotion. Bracing himself, he stepped inside the hospital room.

The former king hadn't requested any special accommodations beyond privacy. There were no flowers or balloons or even cards to add color to the sterile space. Just an assortment of machines and IVs and other medical equipment all too familiar to Carlos, but somehow alien in the context of keeping Enrique Medina alive.

His powerful father was confined to a single bed.

Wearing paisley pajamas, Enrique needed a shave. That alone relayed how ill the old man was even more than his pallor. Even on a secluded island with no kingdom to rule, the deposed monarch had always been meticulous about his appearance.

His father had also lost weight since Carlos's brief visit a couple of months ago for Antonio's wedding. Still stinging from his screwup with Lilah, Carlos hadn't been much in the mood for making merry at a wedding. He'd done his family duty then promptly left with the excuse of a patient in need.

"Mi hijo." A sigh rattled Enrique's chest, and he adjusted the plastic tubes feeding oxygen into his nose. His voice was frail, with only a hint of the authority he'd once carried in booming tones.

"Padre." He swapped to Spanish effortlessly. His father had always spoken their native language with Carlos most often of his sons.

Carlos unhooked the chart from the foot of his father's bed and thumbed through it. "What is this nonsense I hear about you rejecting surgery?"

"I will not survive the operation." Enrique waved dismissively, IV clanking against the metal pole. "I will not put anyone's, most especially my child's, life at risk on such a remote chance."

Looking up from the dire vital stats in front of him in black-and-white, he met his father's eyes unflinchingly. "You're quitting?"

"You are a doctor," he said with a pride Carlos couldn't remember hearing before. Their father had railed at each of his sons for leaving the safety of the island for a wide-open world where any nutcase could assassinate them too. "You have read my chart. You can see how weakened I am. I do not have the will to fight any longer."

Carlos hung the chart carefully on the bed, suppressing the urge to fling the lot across the room in rage. "Listen to me, old man," he bit out carefully. "When I begged you to let me end the pain, you refused. You added more nurses and guards to watch me, to push more treatments and physical therapy and any extreme measures you could find to keep me alive, then get me on my feet again."

Memories of this place, of the torturous rehab sessions he'd endured bombarded him. Of the months in body casts and traction. Of surgery after surgery, pins and steel rods implanted inside him only to be replaced again the next time he grew. And always, the pain, which he could have handled had it not been for the pity stamped on the faces of his caregivers.

He'd finally insisted on solitude whenever possible, gritting through one minute at a time.

"So I will say to you now what you said to me then in the room just next door." He leaned in until they were nearly nose to nose. "You will not give up. A Medina does not surrender."

His father didn't even blink. "It is out of my hands."

"Idiota," Carlos exploded, spinning away and damn near falling on his ass in the process. He grabbed a utility sink for balance, dragging in heaving breaths.

"Carlos," his father's voice ordered with threads of the younger ruler resonating. "I did not bring you up to be disrespectful."

"According to your timetable, I am only days away from becoming the head of this family." The king of nowhere. "So who is going to stop me from saying what I think? Certainly not you."

His father nodded with approval. "You have become tougher over the years."

"I am like you, then."

"Actually, your mother was the truly strong one. But even she could not push me to change my mind."

Mentions of his dead mother stabbed through the last of Carlos's shaky control. "Your plan now isn't any better than your plan then."

"My intent now is as it was then." Enrique's voice faltered. "To protect my children."

Carlos clutched the bed rail in a death grip. "Then don't make us bury another parent prematurely."

The hospital room went silent as his father's pale face turned downright chalky. But damn it all, Carlos would do whatever it took to make his father agree to that transplant.

This life had already stolen too much from their family too early. Unless he persuaded his father to fight, no surgery would stand even a chance of saving him.

A way to tether their father's will more firmly into this world whispered through his brain, a way to have it all. And, yes, he would be manipulating his father in order to keep Lilah, but if that protected both of them? Safeguarded both his father and Lilah? The choice was obvious.

"Stick around and you'll get to meet your grandchild. Your heir."

Regret creased Enrique's weary, weathered face. "Eloisa—"

"I am not talking about her child." He cut his father short. "You'll have to hang on longer than a few weeks for the baby I'm referring to." He took a deep breath in preparation for making that final step and found it easier than he expected. "I've brought someone to the island to meet you—Lilah. She and I are expecting a baby."

Shock, then a deep sadness creased his father's face.

"Son, I am not so ill that I have forgotten your medical history."

"Doctors can be wrong in their dire predictions and hopeless odds." The possibility did exist. Regardless, he would raise her child as his. "And I am living proof. My child is living proof."

He only had to convince Lilah to marry him.

His father's eyes went wide—then watery with emotion. Carlos gathered up his tattered self-control, angry with himself for losing it earlier. Everything was too close to the surface in this place—the island, the clinic.

As much as he ached to be with Lilah tonight, to bury himself in the warm softness of her body, he couldn't risk it. The next time he faced her, he had to have his game plan prepared. If she caught him unaware now, he would combust.

Ten

Lilah bolted upright in her bed.

She searched the dark room lit only by moonbeams piercing the curtains, momentarily disoriented at being in a strange space and unsure what had woken her. The room felt empty, no sounds other than the rolling gush of waves outdoors. She rubbed the slight curve of her stomach as if she could somehow apologize to her baby for disturbing her—his?—slumber as well.

Swinging her feet to the floor, she toe-searched along the dense nap of the antique rug until she found her fuzzy slippers. Eyes adjusting to the darkness, she slid from the high bed, curious and now completely awake. Her sleep had been restless anyway, her imagination painting too vivid a picture of a younger Carlos and his brothers escaping San Rinaldo.

But she refused to get sucked into this extravagant

lifestyle simply because her heart hurt for this family. As much as she truly enjoyed beautiful things, she felt stronger in her own world, where hard work had bought every object in her possession.

She flicked on the bedside lamp, the flood of light confirming she was alone. Where was Carlos now? Asleep in his room on the other side of the sitting area? She hadn't even been able to ask him about what Eloisa had shared. Carlos and his brothers had stayed late at the hospital, visiting with their father. Duarte had called Shannon, who'd passed along the message to the rest of them. Lilah had tried to hide the sting of hurt over Carlos not phoning her directly…then mentally kicked herself for being selfish. He had overwhelming family concerns. This wasn't a pleasure trip.

Still, he could have at least said good-night when he returned.

Snagging her white cotton robe from the bench at the end of her bed, she slipped her arms into the sleeves, covering her matching eyelet nightgown. Carlos's suite was decorated far more starkly than the other quarters she'd seen, much as his Tacoma home provided a bare essentials place to crash. All burgundy leather, deep mahogany wood and brown tones, the space shouted masculinity without even hints of softness to welcome a woman.

As she padded away from her four-poster bed toward the sitting area, she felt the floor vibrate under her bare feet. Again. Again. From music?

She tipped her head to the side, listening more closely to nuances underneath the crash of waves. She swung open the hall door. Melodic runs of a piano swelled from the east wing.

She considered stepping back into her room—or waking up Carlos. But her pride kept her from entering his room when he hadn't bothered to speak to her when he came in.

She stepped farther into the hall. Curious. And determined to tap into her practical lawyer side to find out who was playing, and playing quite masterfully. Nodding to a guard, she continued her search. Hadn't Shannon said she once taught music? If the woman couldn't sleep either, perhaps they could talk more, or she could simply listen until she grew groggy again.

Softly, she followed the hall around corners and down stairs until she stopped outside the almost closed door leading to... She peered inside the circular ballroom she'd only viewed briefly during her tour earlier. Wooden floors stretched across with a coffered ceiling that added texture as well as sound control. Crystal chandeliers and sconces cast shimmering patterns. She looked past the gilded harp to a Steinway grand...

And Carlos?

Not Shannon.

Curiosity melded into something deeper, something more emotional. He sat on the simple black piano bench, his suit jacket and tie discarded over the harp. His gabardine pants were still creased perfectly, a sure sign he hadn't been anywhere near a bed since returning from the hospital.

His face intent, distant, he leaned over the keyboard, his fingers flying across the ivories, playing something classical. Flowing from Carlos's fingertips, the music sounded intense, haunting, so much so she felt the first sting of tears at the tortured passion he milked from every note.

Her feet drew her deeper into the room to a tapestry wingback tucked in a shadowy corner by a stained glass window. She felt closer to him, to the man inside, in this moment than ever before. There were no walls between them now, only raw emotion from someone who'd faced the worst life could dish out and was clawing his way back to the light note by note.

Carlos's hands stilled as the final chord faded. Her breath hitched somewhere between her lungs and throat. She wasn't sure how long she'd been holding it, but hesitated to even exhale for fear of disrupting the mood.

Turning his head slowly, he looked at her over his shoulder. "Sorry to have disturbed you. You were sleeping so soundly when I looked in on you."

He'd come to her room? How long had he watched her? The thought stirred her, knowing he hadn't simply turned in. He'd been concerned, checking, letting her rest. She closed the distance between them with a half-dozen hesitant steps, her slippers whispering across the hardwood floors.

"You didn't bother me. I couldn't sleep," she lied, tracing the curved edge of the Steinway. "How did I never know you played?"

He turned on the wooden bench, his eyes tracking her every movement. "It never came up in conversation. I'm not what you would call chatty."

"That's an understatement." She stared back from the far end of the piano.

Awareness vibrated from him to her like another chord from his fingers.

"What do you want to know, Lilah?"

"Who's your favorite composer?"

"That's it? Your big question?" His bark of laughter cut through the otherwise silent room.

"That's a start."

"Rachmaninoff."

"And you picked him because…?" She walked slowly around the piano toward him again. "Come on, help me out here. Conversation involves more than clipped answers."

"My mother played the piano. He was her favorite to play when she was upset or angry." His fingers hammered out a series of angry chords, then segued into something softer. "When I'm at the piano I can still hear the sound of her voice."

His answer stole the air from her lungs. For a stark man, sometimes he said the most profoundly moving things.

She sat beside him on the bench. "That's beautiful, Carlos. And more than a little heartbreaking."

"Keep up comments like that and I'll stop the sharing game." He picked up the pace until his fingers flew across the keyboard again. "Maybe we can play a game I like to call 'Strip for Secrets'."

She covered his hands with hers, stilling him, the sound fading. "Or you could stop with the games all together and simply talk to me about what's upsetting you. How was your visit with your father?"

"His condition remains unchanged."

Upsetting to be sure, but somehow she hadn't reached the core of what was bothering him, of why he chose to play…. "You're thinking of your mother, maybe?"

As tempted as she was to say to hell with it all and lose herself in his arms, she needed something more first. She needed answers to understanding the man she was considering linking her life with.

The thought stopped her short. She was actually considering his marriage proposal, waiting for a sign that she could trust the feelings building inside her. She waited, letting him find his way as she'd learned long ago there was no pushing this stubborn man into saying or doing anything until he was good and ready.

His hand gravitated back to the keys, rippling a five-finger scale back and forth. "Mother was an artist in a thousand ways and in no way formal. She played the piano by ear. She was an amazing cook but said she learned from watching her mother. And needlework…in spite of having unlimited funds, she knitted blankets."

The low rumble of his voice carried shades of grief, loss and nostalgia in the treasured memories of a lost loved one.

Her heart squeezed with sympathy. "She sounds like a very talented and busy woman."

"Busy?" His eyebrows pinched together. "I never thought of it that way since she was always laid-back, never seemed rushed. But what you say fits with what I remember."

She linked her fingers with his. "How old were you when she died?"

"Thirteen." His squeezed her hand, tightly, the line of his jaw taut. "I prefer to celebrate the way she lived, not dwell on how she died."

Cradling his face, she stroked until the tensed tendons under her fingers eased. "I'm sure she would prefer you treasure those happier memories."

The silence between them stretched with only the

sound of their breathing to fill the vastness of the room and the depth of his loss.

His throat moved in a long swallow before he continued, "I play to remember her because there aren't any home videos or even that many photos of our life as a family. Our father kept us out of the public eye even then as much as he could. He destroyed most of our personal items before we left."

And his life had continued in that stripped-down fashion from his bare-bones office to his stark home… even his place here, understated in comparison to the rest of the opulent mansion. The escape from San Rinaldo had marked this family in so many ways, but Carlos bore physical scars as well.

"Your brothers mentioned gunshot wounds this afternoon. So there wasn't a riding accident."

He shook his head, his answer slower this time. "I was wondering what you would think when that was mentioned earlier."

"Do you want to tell me what happened?"

"You could just access my medical records," he joked lightly.

"Leaving aside the ethics for a moment," she answered seriously, "I wouldn't break your trust that way."

"Ah, Lilah…" He tucked a knuckle under her chin, calluses warm and masculine against her tender skin. "That's why I like you. And believe me, I don't say that lightheartedly."

"Then thank you." She leaned into his hand, deepening the touch, the connection. "I like you, too, most of the time, anyway. Help me understand you so I can like you even more of the time."

He looked away, staring into the open top of the grand

piano at the lines of strings. "I was shot in the back by rebels during our escape from San Rinaldo."

She'd guessed as much from what his brother said earlier, but hearing Carlos confirm it brought the reality of that attack so horribly alive in her mind. "I'm so sorry. I can't even begin to imagine how terrifying and painful that must have been for you."

Still he stared into the piano, his fingers stroking over the ivories without pressing. "Not any more frightening than the kids I treat who've been gunned down in their own neighborhood for no reason other than where they live or what color shirt they wore that day."

He had a point, not that it lessened the horror of what he'd endured. "I guess not."

"I tried to save my mother and I failed. If I'd stepped more to the left… I've replayed that day in my mind so many times and there seem to be a million options I could have taken."

Heartbroken for the young boy he'd been, for the man now, she touched his arm lightly, squeezing the tensed muscle gently. "You were only thirteen."

"At the time I thought I was a man." He glanced at her, his bicep flexing under her touch.

"You must have grown up far too fast that day." Her heart hurt at the image stamped in her mind.

"Stop. I don't want your pity, and I don't want to talk about this anymore."

She flattened her hands to the hard wall of his chest, his heart hammering through his shirt. "How can I know this about you and not be moved? How can I just let it go on command?"

Her defenses were impossible to find, much less resurrect around him. She had to face the fact that it was impossible to stay logical and impartial around Carlos. He pulled her closer until the heat blasting from his body seared through her nightgown, through her skin, deep inside and pooling low.

His head lowered until his breath fanned over her face. "I'll just have to distract you, then."

Smoothly, his mouth covered hers with the familiarity of lovers who knew each other well, who knew just how to touch, stroke, taste and nip to drive the other to the edge. Even just when to hold back and draw that pleasure tighter.

How could a man know her body so well, yet still be such a mystery? She reassured herself that she'd learned more tonight. They were making headway. He'd opened up more tonight than ever before.

And those marriage proposals?

She still didn't know what prompted him to make those offers for a lifetime commitment, but right now, she wanted to focus on the feelings, the connection. Her heart ached for him and all he'd been through. While she refused to let that blind her, she also couldn't look away.

He skimmed aside the shoulder on her robe and gown, exposing her collarbone to his kisses, his hand curving around her breast.

She wasn't as adept as him at shuttling aside tumultuous emotions. So many roiled inside her, she needed an outlet. And regardless of what tomorrow held, she couldn't leave him here alone with his painful memories. "I think it's time to lock that door."

Need for Lilah searing through him, Carlos opened the security panel in the wall beside the door. Every room in the house was equipped with one, a way to lock the doors and seal the windows from any outside intrusion. While his father had installed such extreme safety measures for their protection against everything from hurricanes to an attack, Carlos had an entirely different purpose in mind.

Tapping in codes with as much speed as he'd played the piano, he secured the door with a click and hiss. The windows then darkened until the ballroom became a luxurious—impenetrable—cocoon.

Lilah, seated on the edge of the piano bench, gasped in surprise. "I had no idea. And no one can see inside?"

"This is my home, my dominion," he declared, sauntering toward her. "No one will disturb us. No one can see us. I would never put you at risk. I will keep you safe, always."

The evening spent talking with his father and his brothers was such a mixed bag of familiar and torturous. There was a hole in their family that had never been filled.

A void because he'd failed to keep his mother safe.

And while he knew in his head that he'd been one thirteen-year-old against a small band of rebels, that didn't stop him from feeling, knowing, he should have been able to do more. He'd lived with the knowledge for years, but tonight the memories flayed him raw. More than ever he needed the forgetfulness he knew he could find in Lilah's arms.

Rising, she faced him without hesitation. Her hands fell on his shoulders and he gathered the soft cotton of her nightgown set in his fists. When he saw her pupils widen with desire, he swept the fabric up and over her head. He sent the gown sailing across the room in a white flag of truce, not surrender.

She stood before him, unflinching, proudly naked. His hands trembled ever so slightly as he reached to touch her. Trembled, for God's sake. He was known for his ever-steady control under even the most stressful and lengthy surgeries. But nothing had tapped his composure as deeply as Lilah, her beautiful body and creamy skin on display for him.

Only him.

Possessiveness spread further through him, growing roots until he knew he could never escape the feeling. And right now it became vitally important to make sure she was every bit as consumed by desire as he was.

Cupping her shoulders, he eased her back to the bench, guiding her further still until she reclined with her legs draped over the end. Her eyes flared with understanding a second before he lowered his head. Nudging her knees apart with his shoulders, he stroked up the insides of her thighs, following with slow, deliberate kisses. Her sighs encouraged him.

Aroused him.

Softly, *deliberately,* he nuzzled her through the thin satin barrier of her panties. The scent of her filled him every time he inhaled, which he wanted to do over and over again because nothing, absolutely nothing rivaled her.

He skimmed aside her panties and…yes…tasted her essence, teased her sweet folds. Her back bowed upward as she mumbled sweetly incoherent requests for more. He hooked his arms under her knees and brought her closer, urging her pleasure higher. She gripped his shoulders, her nails cutting half-moons into his flesh. Each husky gasp came faster until she grasped his hair.

"Now," she demanded, "I need you inside me."

No need to tell him twice. "Lucky for us both that's exactly where I want to be."

Kissing her slickened, swollen sex gently once, he eased her feet to the ground again. He stole a lingering look at her, reveling in her dazed eyes, flushed cheeks and tousled hair streaming an auburn flame over the edge of the bench. She'd never looked more beautiful.

She arched upward and he caught her around the waist, shifting her onto the keyboard in a jangled chord. She yanked at his pants with frantic hands, tearing at his zipper until she freed his throbbing length. Bracing his hand behind her on the piano, he thrust inside. Her moist heat clamped around him in sync with her legs locked around his waist. Her heels dug into his buttocks as he thrust again and again.

Their speeding hearts, breaths and sighs mixed with the Steinway's own tune. He let her transport him from this room, from the island and the memories slamming into him from all directions. With each incredible grip of her silken body, stroke of her hands, he realized he'd approached things all wrong with Lilah. He'd thought by shutting her out he could avoid the past. Instead, with Lilah like this, the hell of it faded to the back of his mind. If he could stay with her, inside her, he could shut the rest out.

She clenched around him as her release built, increased until she flung her head back. Her cry of pleasure echoed into the domed ceiling. Hearing her, watching her—feeling her—unravel in his arms snapped the last thread of restraint in him. He pulsed inside her, deeply, fully, and somehow nowhere near enough because already he wanted her again.

Holding her as aftershocks snapped through him, he gathered her close and sank to the piano bench with her in his lap. He smoothed her hair and whispered along her brow how much she moved him, other words he couldn't form or remember, except that some poet inside him had come to life with her.

The feel of her against him, perspiration slicking her skin and sealing her to him, felt so damn right. He skimmed his hands down her back and soaked in the leisurely pleasure of her pressed to him, her breasts, her hips… Her stomach curved ever so slightly and he realized… Her pregnancy was beginning to show. Medically, he knew all the stages and changes she would undergo. But for the first time, he allowed himself to think of experiencing that miracle in an up close and personal way.

As a father.

Something shifted inside him and he slid a hand between them, splaying across her stomach, her child. He felt the weight of her gaze on him and looked up. She stared back with an open vulnerability that sucker punched him. In that moment, she was his old friend, his lover now, the soon-to-be mother of his child, and he had to have her.

The warmth in her eyes all but unraveled him. But he couldn't lose focus, not when he needed her in his life for so many reasons.

He would do anything, say anything, pretend to be the man she seemed to want if that's what it took to persuade her to stay.

Eleven

Lounging in the overlarge tub in her suite, Lilah leaned back against Carlos's chest. His long legs stretched on either side of hers with rose petals floating in the water, scenting the air. She'd never seen a place with so many fresh flowers around every corner, even vases alongside the LCD screen and sound system currently piping Beethoven into their tiled retreat.

Two brandy snifters filled with milk sat on a silver platter beside the marble tub. He'd insisted that if she couldn't drink alcohol, then he would abstain as well. The silly gesture touched her as fully as his hands.

He'd made such intense love to her in the music room, and again in her bed before they'd migrated to the spacious bath. Her wary heart wondered if maybe, just maybe, she could trust what they shared. Hopefully he'd resolved whatever freaked him out that first night they'd been together. Without question, Carlos carried heavy baggage from his past. That had to have left some emotional marks.

But as long as they kept open lines of communication, maybe they really had a shot at working this out. Counting on that honesty between them calmed her own fears of ending up like her parents. It had to. Because heaven help her, if Carlos asked her to marry her again, she wouldn't be able to say no.

He swept his foot under the brass faucet, activating the electronic fixture. Warm water flowed into their cooling bath.

What would she have done if he'd proposed right after she told him about the baby? Her hand tightened on his knee. She liked to think she would have told him to take his dutiful proposal and shove it after the way he'd acted. She needed—and deserved—confirmation that he held deep feelings for her, not just because she carried his baby.

Nestled against his chest, she wanted to roll out her thoughts, test their newfound truce, but concerns for his father had to take precedence. No wonder he'd been pouring his heart out through his music.

She stroked up his leg and reached through the rose-covered surface of the water, folding her hand over his cupping the snifter. "The way you played—" her fingers caressed the rougher texture of his "—your hands on the keyboard, it was magical. You're quite accomplished."

"There wasn't much else for me to do during my teenage years. Between surgeries…" His voice rumbled his chest against her back, his low words mingling with the sound of water shooshing from the faucet. "My father had the music room built to be airy, open and bright, like being outside."

"Apparently you spent a lot of time practicing." Pouring out his pain, his loss, his frustration onto the keyboard? What a heart-wrenching image.

"More than average." He brought the goblet of milk to her mouth for a sip. "One especially hot July day, my brothers surprised me by showing up with wheelchairs they'd lifted from the island clinic. They nailed a basketball goal right in the middle of one of our father's murals and gave 'ballroom' a whole new meaning."

She tried to laugh with him, but her mind hitched on one telling word. "Wheelchairs? You were in a wheelchair?"

With careful deliberation, he swept his foot under the electronic sensor again and shut off the water. "For a while, the doctors weren't sure whether or not I would walk again."

"How long is awhile?" she pressed gently.

"Three years before I was on my feet again. Seven more years of surgeries after that." He reached for his milk abruptly and drained the glass.

"Carlos..." she gasped, at a loss, overwhelmed by what he must have gone through. "I had no idea." She tried to turn, to face him, to comfort him, but he locked her in place with one arm around her.

He set aside his snifter and slid his hand over her stomach. "Let's talk about something else instead. You're learning a lot of my crummy past. How about you share up some things about yourself?"

"Strip for Secrets doesn't work when we're already naked."

"I have plenty of other enticements to offer." His

hand dipped below the water, between her legs for a languorous caress.

His obvious attempt to change the subject didn't escape her notice—even though it was growing difficult to think of anything but the talented tease of his fingers.

She angled back to kiss his jaw. "What do you want to know?"

Laughing softly, he moved his hand to her stomach again. "Are you hoping for a boy or girl?"

And, wow, he'd chosen his distracting topic well, because finally they were talking about their child in a way she'd barely dared dream.

"I haven't thought about that one way or the other." She held his hand over her stomach just as she'd done earlier around the goblet of milk. "The baby already is what he or she is."

His fingers circled lightly along her skin. "Are you planning to find out during the ultrasound?"

"It doesn't matter to me either way." She forced herself to relax, to grow comfortable with his hand curving over her stomach as if it belonged there. "Are you hoping for a boy?"

Just yesterday he'd said he wanted the baby to be his. Was he finally settling into the reality of being a father after all? She could see how he would have grown leery of hope after such traumatic teenage years. At the hospital, she'd witnessed more than one patient become cynical to the point of losing reasonable perspective.

If only she'd known more about Carlos's past from the start.

His deep inhale pressed against her back before he

finally answered, "I don't have any preferences other than that the child be healthy."

"We're in agreement on that." She swirled her fingers through the water, swirling red petals before her hand fell to rest on top of his again. "Well then, do you have name preferences?"

"The Medinas typically pull from the family tree."

Everything she'd learned since coming to the island had shed such light, helping her understand this enigmatic man. Did she dare push further? Yet, how could she not when this could be her only window of time? "Your mother's name was Beatriz, right?"

"She didn't care much for her name. She said it sounded too old-fashioned."

"And what about boy names?"

"My family tree is filled with relatives. We have plenty to choose from."

We? Her heart raced against her ribs. "We'll have to make a list."

"What about your family?" He skimmed a kiss across her temple, brushing aside a stray curl that had fallen from the loose bundle on her head. "Any names you wish to use?"

The water went chilly again. "Not really." She toed the drain to release some water and activated the brass faucet again, grateful for what had to be the world's largest hot water tank. "We aren't estranged or anything. My brothers and I keep in touch, but we're not what I would call close. We exchange emails, speak a couple of times a year. I try to make it for special occasions in my nieces' and nephews' lives. But we're not all taking family vacations together by any stretch."

"You've done an admirable job in setting up what

works best for everyone," he said, his tone non-judgmental, another characteristic she liked about him. "Have you told your family about the baby yet?"

"My parents are away on their fifteenth honeymoon."

"Fifteenth anniversary? I didn't realize you had a stepparent."

"No, you heard correctly." She really didn't want to think about this now, but she'd demanded so much from him tonight. She owed him the same consideration. "They're both my biological parents, and it's their fifteenth honeymoon, not fifteenth anniversary. You've heard of couples rekindling the romance with a second honeymoon? Well, my parents are on their fifteenth reconciliation."

"Sounds like they've had a rocky go of it," he offered up another diplomatic answer.

"That's putting things mildly." She sat upright, hugging her knees, all of a sudden weary of dancing around the truth. "My father cheats. My mother forgives him. They go on an elaborately romantic getaway that puts stars back in my mother's eyes until the next time he strays and the cycle starts all over again."

His strong arms went around her, muscles twitching with restraint as he held her gently. "They've hurt you."

"In the past? Yes. Now I'm mostly…numb, I guess you could say." She rested her cheek against his forearm. "When it comes to the two of them, nothing surprises me anymore."

"That's why you were so upset when you bumped into Nancy outside my office."

"And don't forget the airport."

He turned off the water and pulled her to her feet in a fluid movement. Facing her dripping wet and naked, water pooling around their toes on the warmed tiles, he stared directly into her eyes. "I may have gone out with her but I never slept with her. You kept getting in the way."

"What do you mean?" She needed to hear him say it, to spell out every single thought as salve for her wounded ego and hope for her wary heart.

Carlos gripped her shoulders in his broad palms. "She's a perfectly nice and attractive woman, but she bored the hell out of me because she wasn't you."

"You're just saying that to get into my good graces." Although right now she wasn't sure why he would work so hard for that. They were already sleeping together again. And, sure, she hadn't agreed to his proposals, but they had time now.

"I'm sorry your father has made it difficult for you to trust what I say." He'd touched too close to the truth, like poking his surgeon finger right into an open wound.

She snatched up a towel from the warming drawer and tucked it tight under her arms. "Don't put this off on him, and don't blame it on some hang-up I may have." She thrust another towel at him, reminded too vividly of when she'd confronted him in the hospital shower. "You are the one who refused to speak to me after the Christmas party."

"I did what I thought was best for you." He knotted the towel over one hip.

"Easier for you, you mean." How had this conversation gone so wrong so fast? Was she sabotaging herself? Scared to take the happiness just an arm's reach away?

"Then let's make this right." He clasped her shoulders

again to keep her from racing away from him. "Forget taking any paternity tests. I accept the baby is mine and I want us to be married. Tomorrow. No more waiting. We can have the ceremony performed in my father's hospital room."

No paternity test?

He believed her.

Finally, she heard the words she'd been hoping for from the beginning. Almost everything. He hadn't said he loved her. But then her father threw the word *love* around like pennies in a fountain. Cheap and easy to come by. Carlos was offering her something far more precious and tangible. He was offering her the truth.

Drawing in a bracing breath, she took the biggest gamble of her life and placed her hand in his. "Call the preacher." As the words fells from her lips, she tried like hell not to think of the morning after they'd made love for the first time nearly three months ago.

Lilah reached for Carlos, called his name softly as she woke…but her hand found nothing but cool cotton sheets and emptiness on his side of the bed. She might have thought the whole crazy night with him after the fundraiser had been a dream. But her body carried reminders of their impetuous lovemaking, from the tender muscles of her legs after their near acrobatics on his office desk to the scent of chlorine in her hair from his hot tub on the deck of his mountainside home.

How appropriate he should live on a cliff, how in keeping with the edginess of the man himself.

She stretched her arms overhead, her eyes adjusting to the dim room lit only with a few pale streaks of morning sun. Not that she could afford to lounge around. In a Tacoma winter it could be nearly eight in the morning already.

Her toes protesting the chilly hardwood floors, she searched for something more appropriate to wear than a sheet or her evening gown currently crumpled in a corner. She'd kicked the designer dress off and away in her frenzy to be with Carlos again, in his bed, then in the hot tub, before returning to his room, certain she was too exhausted for more. Only to have him prove her wrong.

A smile on her lips, she plucked his tuxedo shirt off the bedside lamp. Apparently she'd thrown his clothes around too. The crisp fabric still carried his scent, stirring her all over again with languid memories of making love until the blend of them together made a sensual perfume.

She found him in his kitchen, another simple room with the bare essentials—stainless steel appliances with black-and-white tiles.

And one hot chef wearing only a low-slung pair of scrubs that showcased his taut butt as perfectly as any tailored tux.

The scent of frying bacon hung in the air as he tended the stove, a second pan in place with batter in a measuring cup.

He pivoted toward her. And with one look at his emotionless eyes, the stark set of his jaw, all the warmth seeped from her. He took in her standing there in his shirt and…nothing. He didn't smile. He didn't reach for her.

Carlos simply turned away. "Do you want breakfast?"

She wanted to tell him to go to hell. Instead she said, "I think it's best if I just go."

Still, like a fool, she hesitated, giving him a chance to say something softer, nicer. Instead, he just opened the refrigerator and pulled out a carton of milk.

Apparently last night had been a dream after all, and it was time for her to wake up....

Unable to sleep, Lilah inched from Carlos's bed, the one in his father's mansion. Although the past and present felt strangely merged at the moment with memories of that wretched morning after hammering in her head.

Careful not to disturb Carlos, she reached into her purse on the bedside table and fished free her cell phone. The scent of roses from their bath filled the room, a much sweeter scent than those chlorine-tinted recollections.

Things were different now, damn it. All the same, she resisted the temptation to crawl under the covers and spoon against his back. She needed to take care of a niggling detail.

Before she surrendered her guard fully to her future husband, she needed to call her parents.

Tiptoeing, she left the room, closing the door softly, before curling up in the window seat to place her call, nerves pattering. She knew they would be happy, but she'd put off the conversation because she had a tough time reconciling herself to a lifetime with a man who had held back from her in so many ways, a man who would never have chosen this life for himself if she hadn't gotten pregnant. She thumbed "seven" on her speed dial and waited through so many rings she almost gave up. Then—

"Hello?" Her mother's voice cut through the static of the distant connection of her parents' "anniversary" cruise. She hadn't been exactly truthful when she'd told Carlos she couldn't call them. It had been one thing to hold the baby news close for a while, another matter to keep an established pregnancy and an impending wedding from her mother.

"Mom, it's me." She hugged her knees, her nightgown draping her legs.

"Lilah, honey, it's so great to hear your voice," her mother said enthusiastically, not even mentioning the hour or how the call must have woken her. "Let me get your father on the phone too."

"Mom, no, really." Her head fell to rest against the warm windowpane. "You don't need to disturb him."

"Don't be silly." Her voice faded as she must have pulled the receiver from her face. "Darren? Darren, wake up. It's Lilah."

Her father's voice rumbled along with the rustle of sheets in their cruise ship cabin. How her parents managed to stay together she couldn't imagine and didn't want to dwell on overlong with her own hastily conceived wedding on the horizon.

"Okay," her mother said, back on the line. "I'm switching you to speakerphone."

"Mornin', pumpkin," her father said groggily.

There wasn't a breath deep enough to prepare her to say the words she never thought she would say to her parents. "Mom, Dad, I'm getting married…."

* * *

His wedding day was overcast, but he was a man of science, not superstition.

Carlos stood by his father's hospital bed in the island clinic, Lilah beside him. His brothers, his sister and their significant others gathered in a corner. Limited visitation rules were out the window for the duration of what promised to be the shortest service on record. A priest waited at the foot of the bed, looking a bit confused as to whether he'd been called for last rites rather than a marriage.

Enrique struggled to sit up straighter. "Are you sure you want to do this?"

Startled, Carlos looked at his father, then realized the old man was speaking to Antonio. The youngest Medina son was the donor match—he would give a lobe of his liver—he would save their father's life. Something Carlos couldn't do in spite of all his medical degrees.

"Absolutely certain," Antonio answered from beside his wife.

Enrique slid the pocket watch from his bedside table. "You used to play with this when you were a boy. I want you to have it. It is a small thing to give you in exchange for a piece of your liver—"

"Thank you. I'll keep it until you're well enough to need it again." Antonio took the watch, swallowing hard before giving his father a brisk but heartfelt hug. "Besides, you pretty much gave me my liver in the first place."

"You are a strange boy." Enrique shook his head, then wheezed for air. His face pale, he continued haltingly, "And Carlos, I have something of yours, *mi hijo.*"

Enrique extended a gnarled hand, a black velvet

box in his grip. Carlos didn't even have to open it to know what rested inside…his mother's wedding rings, a platinum diamond set, meant to be worn by a queen. Meant to be worn by Lilah. He was still stunned she'd actually agreed.

The wary hope in her eyes when she'd said yes made him feel like a first-class ass. He wasn't the romantic hero she dreamed of. He wasn't wired that way, a flaw in himself he'd known from the start. But it was too late to protect her from that any longer. They were tied to each other through the fragile life inside her, and he would do his best to make sure she never realized the bad deal she'd made. Taking the box from his father, Carlos turned to Lilah with a king's ransom worth of gems in his hand.

Twelve

Lilah twisted the platinum diamond ring set around and around on her finger, hardly able to process all that had happened in the past thirty-six hours since she and Carlos had exchanged "I Dos" at the island clinic. Now, she and most of the Medinas paced in a private waiting area at the Jacksonville hospital where Enrique had been transferred for his transplant.

While she wasn't a big fan of preferential treatment, she understood how much mayhem their presence would have caused had they been placed in the public waiting area. The Medina fame should not intrude on someone else's crisis.

And she had to admit the quiet for their own emergency was helpful. Her nerves were fried. In her job as a hospital administrator, she'd witnessed so many families facing similar ordeals, but she'd never been on this side of the surgery.

Tests, doctors, plans had filled the past day and a half to the point of exhaustion. For the two nights prior, she and Carlos had made intense love before falling asleep. Any honeymoon plans, even any talking would have to wait. Right now their world was tightly focused into these four walls, with antiseptic air and bad coffee.

The door opened and Antonio's wife, Shannon, walked into the waiting room. She'd been sitting with her husband as he awaited surgery. "Enrique would like to see you."

Carlos, Duarte and Eloisa stood in sync from the steel and pleather sofa.

"No..." Shannon shook her head. "He wants to see Lilah."

Surprise held her still as a Red Cross volunteer pushed a cart full of books and magazines past the open door.

"Me?" Lilah asked. "Are you sure?"

"Absolutely," Shannon said, tucking a limp strand of blond hair back into her hair clamp.

Carlos, her *husband*—how strange that word still felt—shot her a quizzical look before squeezing her hand with encouragement. Standing, she smoothed her dress. While she'd met Enrique just before the surreal wedding ceremony in his room at the island clinic, there hadn't been much time for "get to know you" chats.

A lump lodged in her chest as she realized this could be her only opportunity to speak to him.

She scrounged for composure as she walked closer to the ICU room in front of the nurse's station. Tapping on the door, she waited, the low murmur of staff mingling with the *beep, beep, beep* of medical equipment.

Through the glass window, she saw the critically ill king with a nurse sitting vigil. Enrique raised a hand, IV taped in place, and waved her into the room weakly.

The nurse excused herself quietly and shifted her post to the hall side of the window. Lilah stepped deeper inside the ICU unit.

"Shannon said you wanted to see me." She wasn't sure what to call him. "Your Majesty" seemed awkward given they were relatives.

"You may call me *Padre,* like my boys do," he said in a raspy voice as if reading her mind. Or perhaps he was just an intuitive man. "Sit."

Sit? She stifled a smile at his brusque order, so like his son. Lilah settled into the chair beside his bed. "What did you wish to speak to me about?"

"You are a lawyer. Look at this." He pointed to a folder on the bedside table.

Curious, confused, she opened the manila folder and found… "Your will?"

"I want you to read over it," he insisted.

Clasping the papers to her chest, she studied his eyes for some clue as to why he'd made such a surprise request. "You must have the best of attorneys. Why are asking me to review it?"

"Do not worry. I am not suffering from diminished capacity," he said with a wry grin, his eyes sharp in spite of his critically ill state.

"Your sense of humor is certainly still intact, even if it is a bit twisted." She tapped the folder. "I will read your will if that's what you wish."

"I do." He nodded once. "And before I go into surgery I want to dictate an amendment. I need you to witness it."

The legalese of a king's last will and testament had to be intense. There hadn't been a class on this in law school, and it wasn't something she'd come across in Tacoma, Washington. "Again, I will advise you that you have attorneys in place who are far better versed in your holdings and unique situation."

"Are you going to ask me about the amendment?"

"You will tell me when you're ready." She pulled the pen clipped to the top of the folder and found a legal pad underneath the typed pages.

"You are a patient woman, a necessary quality when dealing with Carlos."

She met and held his eyes. "I hope your decision to have the surgery gives you both a second chance."

"He did not leave me much choice when he told me about the baby you are carrying. I never thought I would live to see Carlos's child." The old man's dark eyes blurred with unshed tears. "While nothing can erase what happened to my Beatriz and to Carlos, there is healing in knowing my decision to send my family away did not cost Carlos everything."

Lilah struggled to process that, but her brain was still stuck on the first part. He knew about the baby? She and Carlos had agreed to wait until after the surgery to tell his family. Hadn't that meant waiting to tell his father too? Perhaps she'd misunderstood Carlos.

And she really hoped she'd misunderstood Enrique.

Ungluing her tongue from the roof of her mouth, she sought clarification. "He told you about the baby to persuade you to have the transplant surgery?"

A smile kicked into one cheek, a laugh rumbling the old monarch's chest until he began coughing. A tear trickled free and he brushed it aside with an impatient swipe. "He certainly did, the very second he set foot on the island. I have to admit I did not think anything could convince me, but Carlos, he is every bit as Machiavellian as his father. Now let us go about writing that child into my will, even though it is my heartfelt hope that I will survive this procedure."

And Carlos hadn't once mentioned to her that he'd twisted the king's arm. If he'd even hinted as much to her—if Carlos had shared anything of his heart and his feelings about his father's grave condition—she might have been able to overlook the fact that he was walling her out emotionally. But she hadn't been given access to Carlos's heart any more than ever. It was like he was still staring at her across that kitchen with the scent of frying bacon in the air and his cold, cold eyes warning her what they shared hadn't meant all that much to him.

As they'd flown to the island, she'd wondered what he wanted from her. Now she knew.

Bottom line, he'd used her.

The wary optimism she'd been feeling since exchanging vows faltered at Enrique's words. Had every one of those proposals been about fulfilling a dying father's wish to see his son settled? About giving Enrique a reason to hang on?

She'd thought the lack of love talk from Carlos meant nothing. That his actions spoke louder. And, sadly, that was true. With Enrique's revelation still fresh on her ears, she knew. Carlos had only married her to ensure his father would have the surgery, that he would fight to live.

How ironic. She wasn't so different from her mother, after all. In spite of all her best intentions she'd allowed herself to be blinded by her feelings for Carlos. And

God, yes, even with hurt and anger coursing through her, she couldn't deny how deeply she loved Carlos Medina. Her husband. The father of her child.

She also couldn't deny the truth staring her in the face. Her marriage was a sham.

Nine hours later, Carlos sagged back in his seat in relief as his father's surgeons left the waiting area. The procedure was a success. Both his father and Antonio were in stable condition. Enrique wasn't out of the woods, but he'd made it over a substantial hurdle.

Eloisa cried tears of relief on her husband's shoulder. Even reserved Duarte was smiling, hugging his fiancée hard. Shannon was already sitting with Antonio in recovery.

Carlos turned to his new bride. Finally, finally, they could celebrate. Her brittle smile gave him pause. Something had been off with Lilah since she'd returned from his father's room. But she'd denied as much, telling him she was simply concerned about Enrique. That they should all focus on the surgery and nothing else. And he had. For nine long, gut-wrenching hours, that had been all he'd thought about.

But with the good news from the king's doctor easing his fears for his father, Carlos now had the clarity to see something was definitely wrong.

She touched his knee lightly. "I'm glad your father and brother both came through so well. If you don't need me anymore, I would like to go back to the hotel."

"You must be tired." He hadn't considered what a physical toll this would take on a pregnant woman. As a doctor, he should have known better. He should have been looking out for her. "Of course. I'll drive you over."

"It's okay." She flinched away from his touch. "I can get there on my own. You stay here where you're needed."

Before he could sort through her words, she started down the tiled corridor, weaving around an aide rolling a laundry cart. What the hell was going on?

She hadn't said anything specific that he could fault. She had every reason in the world to be exhausted. But in the short span of their marriage, not once had she left his side without a kiss. A squeeze of his hand. Some gesture of warmth he'd already grown accustomed to. Now, something in her eyes shouted anger.

Hurt.

And he'd seen that look in her eyes before, a little less than three months ago. She'd stepped into his kitchen—wearing his shirt and looking so damn right in his clothes, in his house, in his life that he'd lost it. He'd shut her out.

Hell. He'd done exactly what he was doing now. He was letting her walk away.

Carlos charged after her, cursing under his breath at his bum leg that made catching her painful and slow.

Finally, he called out, bracing a hand against the hall wall. "Lilah? Lilah, stop."

She slowed and turned silently beside the gleaming stained glass of the hospital chapel door.

Limping, he closed the distance between them in the deserted late-night corridor. "What's really going on here?"

"Just what I said." She folded her arms over her chest,

pulling her cotton dress tighter over her full breasts. "I'm returning to the hotel."

"Wait and I'll come with you," he repeated his offer from earlier.

"There's no need to pretend anymore, Carlos." Her voice was low and tight, her emerald eyes so sad they sliced right through him. "I'm not going to spill the beans to a critically ill man."

Unease scratched at his gut. "I'm not sure I understand what you mean."

Blinking fast, she looked around impatiently, then tugged him into the chapel. Her eyes glinted with a deep hurt. "Your father told me how you persuaded him to get the surgery. How you gave him hope with this baby."

He couldn't deny what she'd said, but he needed to figure out something to diffuse the sadness radiating off her. "Is it so wrong to want to do whatever it takes to give my father a reason to live?"

"Whatever it takes?" She laughed once but her face was devoid of any humor. "We shouldn't have this discussion now. We're both wiped out, and you should be with your family."

"I'm here with you."

"For how long?" She stopped short and held up her hands, a row of candles behind her casting a glow around her. "Forget I said that."

"No," he said tightly. Yes, he'd maneuvered the situation, but in a way that was best for everyone. "We got married, and pardon me if I don't see where that makes me a bad guy."

She backed away from him, deeper into the dimly lit chapel. "I blame myself, too, you know. I was so gullible in believing your quick turnaround in accepting the baby. I mean really, it's only been what? Less than a week since I confronted you in your office and you denied your own child."

Her tearful words pierced through bit by bit until he realized… "You actually believe I had some ulterior motive for marrying you?"

"Your father refuses to have surgery, then you magically give him a reason to live, thanks to this life inside me that you've never felt any connection to at all." She clutched the end of a wooden pew.

He couldn't even refute her. She was a woman of honor and he'd treated her so dishonorably he was ashamed. He'd thrown away this chance to have a life with the child he'd never thought he would have and the loss gutted him. This offspring would be an even greater miracle than his recovering the use of his legs, and instead of doing everything in his power to ensure that child's future, he'd spent the last week driving away the woman who carried his legacy.

"Lilah, I'm sorry," he said simply, sincerely.

"Well, Carlos." She backed away. "You're a little too late, because I'm not so sure I can believe you anymore."

Stunned by the way the day had gone sour so quickly, he watched her turn away, clearly dismissing him. Leaving him with no room for doubt.

His new bride had dumped him.

As Carlos's uneven footsteps faded, Lilah sank onto a wooden pew, her legs giving out. She raked her wrist under her nose, sniffling up the tears and getting a noseful of scented smoke from the half-dozen candles burning by the door. Had she really just tossed away her husband of two days?

She'd kept her silence during the surgery and had planned to wait before packing her bags. Except Carlos had pressed her until the words fell out, until finally she was honest with him the way she should have been right from the start. She never should have stayed silent for months.

What a mess she'd made of her life. She thumbed the wedding set around and around on her finger, the beautiful rings that had come with such hope. A family heirloom that also cost a fortune and didn't belong to her. She needed to return it before she left the hospital.

Stretching her legs out on the pew, she studied the diamonds sparkling as they caught and reflected the stained glass windows. She stared until her eyes grew heavy and closed as sleep drew her in. This time, she knew there wouldn't be any dreams of Carlos waiting to greet her.

The argument with Lilah still reverberating in his head, Carlos watched his baby brother sleep, sitting vigil to give his sister-in-law a break. Sure, Antonio was only eight years younger, but Carlos still saw the kid he'd been when they left San Rinaldo. Carlos held the gold pocket watch in his hand, turning it over and over, remembering another night when their father had given Antonio the antique. They'd been preparing to leave San Rinaldo, and Enrique had told his youngest son to safeguard the timepiece until they met up again.

That long ago day, Antonio had clutched it while wrapping himself in that pewter-colored afghan, telling his brothers the blanket was his shield. The watch was his treasure. He'd been a child trying to find a frame of reference for the unimaginable.

Then the attack had come just two blocks before they reached the ship that was supposed to carry them away from San Rinaldo. They'd been in a park, such a benign place. Duarte and Antonio had thought they were deep in a forest, but their childish minds had misperceived. They'd been so small, everything must have appeared larger than from Carlos's teenage perspective.

Still, when the attack had started, he'd told Duarte to watch over Antonio. And he, as the oldest, would protect their mother. Duarte had succeeded. Carlos had failed. Now, Antonio had saved their father. The baby boy of the Medina family wasn't so little anymore. Antonio filled the bed with his bulk, an avid outdoorsman even now that he could kick back in an office if he so chose.

They'd all come a long way since that nightmare escape from San Rinaldo. Yet, at the moment, he could have sworn he was still stuck there, in that day, with a home and family he could never have back.

Was it any wonder he'd screwed up so badly with Lilah?

His brother's eyes opened heavily, cutting short maudlin thoughts.

Carlos forced a smile and placed the watch on the end table by a cup of ice chips. "Welcome back."

"Our father?" he croaked out, rustling the sheets with slow shifting, followed by a wince.

"Is fine. Resting comfortably. As you should be doing." Carlos passed the cup of ice shavings to dampen Antonio's mouth until his doctor gave the okay for drinking again. "You, my brother, look like hell."

"Is that any way to talk to the guy who saved the day?" Antonio joked in a raspy voice.

"Ah, now I know you're all right."

"Damn straight." He laughed, then coughed with another wince. "Thanks for sitting with me, but don't you have a new bride to spend time with?"

"She's, uh, resting at the hotel."

Antonio's eyebrow shot up, his gaze unexpectedly clear. Canny. Too damn shrewd. "You're a really crummy liar."

"And you're a crummy patient." He passed his brother a small pillow. "Hold this against your incision when you cough. Coughing is good, expands your lungs and keeps you from getting pneumonia. Practice while I find Shannon." He started to stand.

Antonio clamped a hand on his wrist, his grip surprisingly strong for a guy who'd just been through major surgery. "What's wrong? And don't dodge. We know each other too well. You go into doctor mode whenever you're uncomfortable."

His baby brother most definitely wasn't a kid anymore. Still, Carlos didn't want to unload his problems on someone in his brother's condition. Although it was unlikely Antonio would even remember given residual anesthesia still seeped through his system.

And hell, he didn't know what to say to Lilah back at the hotel anyhow.

Carlos sank back into his seat. "Lilah thinks I married her just to make our father have the surgery."

"Did you?" Antonio asked. "I'm not judging. Just wondering."

"Partly. But not fully." Carlos looked at his clasped

hands. "She's pregnant. Apparently I'm not shooting blanks anymore."

"Congratulations, my brother." He raised a fist, woozily, but steady enough to be bumped by Carlos's fist in salute. "So I'm guessing you forgot to tell her you love her. It might not be obvious to the world at large, but to your family it's apparent how far gone you are for her."

His eyes slammed shut. Of course he was. Of course he had been since that morning after the fundraiser when he'd run scared from how Lilah tore down walls inside him, how she forced him to step out of the shadows of the past and face the future. Face the risk of loving, of possibly losing that person.

Because, hell yes, he loved her, with a fierceness that rocked him.

"Far gone? That I am." He couldn't avoid the truth in his brother's words. "What makes you think I botched the proposal?"

"You're a brilliant surgeon and a gifted musician, but when it comes to words?" Antonio shook his head on the pillow. "The years you spent in the hospital cost you communication skills."

Carlos resisted the urge to snap a sarcastic comment. He'd had enough of people raking him over the coals for one day. Standing, he glanced at his brother's vitals, happy to distance himself with the role of doctor. "You should rest."

"And you should listen to me." His gravelly voice carried an undeniable authority. "Women like to hear the words. Unless you are afraid to say it."

Carlos raised an eyebrow. "Calling me a chicken isn't going to work. We're not kids on a playground."

"Granted…" Antonio paused for another cough. "But I can't forget the way it motivated me."

"Pardon?" Was the anesthesia making his brother incoherent? If so, did that mean he could disregard the love advice too?

Antonio set aside the pillow. "That day we were leaving San Rinaldo."

"I still don't know what you mean." His memories of that day were full of blood and pain. "I just remember… Mother."

His brother nodded shortly, his face creased with an agony that clearly had nothing to do with incisions or surgery. "But after she died, you got us out of there. You kept us going, even told me to stop being a chicken and move my ass. Duarte and I would have died without you that day." The steady beep of his heartbeat on the monitor filled the silence as he swallowed another ice chip. "I understand it chaps your hide that you weren't the one to give an organ to save our dad. But, hell, Carlos, you can't be the hero all the time. It doesn't hurt to be a regular guy every now and again."

He hadn't thought of it in quite those terms, but his brother's words resonated. Since their escape, he'd been trapped in the past. Trying to save others, save his father, somehow erase the time he'd failed to save his mother. He'd allowed that day to put a wall between him and moving forward with a normal life.

And he'd allowed that wall to block him from seeing what was right in front of his face—an amazing woman to love. He loved Lilah Anderson Medina, and the time had come to not only show her, but to tell her.

And he wouldn't stop until she believed him.

* * *

Lilah was certain she must be dreaming. Otherwise, how could she be looking into a face full of love?

But the hard church pew hurting her hip felt uncomfortably real enough. She blinked fast to clear her eyes and still Carlos sat beside her, his arms crossed as if he'd been waiting for her to wake. The scent of knotty pine pervaded the chapel. The warm wood walls and rafters remained unvarnished, reminding her of the cabin in Vail where she and Carlos had started this journey.

Sitting up, she scraped her hair back from her face. "Carlos? How long have you been here? Is everything all right with your father and Antonio?"

It must be okay or he wouldn't look so…at peace. "Everyone is fine, all asleep in fact. It's been a long few days. But that's no excuse for the way I handled things with you."

Her heart tripped over itself, but she couldn't allow herself to turn to mush. She needed something more from him this time. She couldn't settle for half measures and avoidance of what really mattered. Her baby deserved better.

She deserved better. "What exactly do you mean?"

"Going to make me work for this, are you? Good for you." He lifted her left hand, thumbing her wedding rings. "I've messed this up from the start, from the way I ran scared from how I felt about you to the way I asked you to marry me. I'm sorry for that. More sorry than can be put into words, but I'm going to try my best."

"Words are good." They both were such workaholic, type A people, neither of them had slowed down long enough to say some important things along the way.

Hope built inside her. She'd slept away some of the anger, enough to listen with a more open heart.

He skimmed a kiss over her knuckles. "I want to be your husband now and always. Not because of my father, but because my life is so empty without you. I will be here for you and our baby every day of my life. I can't promise not to brood, but I vow to share all those brooding thoughts."

The deep tone of commitment in his voice, in his words, bowled her over. This was so much more than she'd ever expected, more than she'd dreamed she might find with such a reserved man.

"Brooding is okay every now and again." She squeezed his hand, encouraging him to continue. After waiting so long for a sign from him, she intended to soak up every second of this.

"I appreciate the way you keep me from sinking too far into that abyss. From losing myself in my work until I'm no good to anyone." His deep voice rumbled low, echoing gently around the empty chapel. "More than my lover, my wife, the mother of my child, you are my friend. You're the one person standing between me and a life of supreme loneliness."

Happy tears clogged her throat for a moment before she could push words free. "Wow, for a man of few words, you're quite poetic when you choose to be. Perhaps some of that artist in you is showing as it does when you play the piano."

"After being scared to death over the thought of losing you, I'm finding it much easier than I expected to be poetic for the woman I love."

Love.

Of all the words he could have chosen, that was the

one she needed to hear most. The one she wasn't sure he would ever voice. But as she looked at the emotion burning strong in his eyes, she didn't doubt him for a second.

"Carlos, I wish I could offer words as beautiful as yours, but right now all I can think about is how relieved I am that we figured this out, that we got it right, because I love you too."

She cradled his face, savoring the bristle of his unshaven cheek, the curve of his smile against her touch. And as she tipped her forehead to his, forging a connection she knew would last a lifetime, she found the right words coming to her. "I adore everything about you, from your brilliant mind to the feel of your hands when we're together. From the way you remember chocolate mint milkshakes to how you devote your life to your patients when you could have so easily taken an easier path." She skimmed her mouth over his, whispering softly against his lips. "You are an amazing man, Carlos Medina, and I look forward to loving you for the rest of my life."

"Exactly what I wanted—but didn't dare hope—to hear." He kissed her deeply, reverently, and the honesty in his touch spoke so clearly she wondered why she hadn't heard it before.

His talented hands stroked down her arms and linked fingers with her. "Will you marry me again?" He gestured to the small, simple altar draped in purple embroidered linens. "Here, now?"

"Of course, my love," she said to her royal lover, her blessedly human husband. "I will. Or rather I should say I do."

Epilogue

Eight months later

Carlos walked the floors of his suite in the island mansion, patting his son's back and singing him to sleep. He wasn't the lullaby sort, but an old Frank Sinatra tune seemed to work just as well. A couple of verses of "Fly Me to the Moon" and the kid was out like a light.

Cradling his seven-week-old sleeping newborn in his hands, Carlos lowered him carefully into the blue eyelet bassinet but didn't—couldn't—step away. Staring at his child had become a favorite pastime of late. Studying the miracle of those perfect hands and feet could keep him mesmerized for a good twenty minutes by this blessing he'd once given up hope of having.

Tiny but long fragile fingers wrapped around Carlos's thumb. "Maybe we've got a future musician in the family with those hands of yours. What do you think, little Enrique?"

Lilah had insisted on naming their child for his grandpa.

The old king had recovered from his transplant surgery with a surprising strength and speed. His will to fight was back in full form so he could walk the beaches with his namesake—and his other new grandchild, Eloisa's daughter, Ginger.

Both infants were so clearly Medinas they looked like brother and sister with their dark hair and stubborn jawlines. Plans were already in place for all the Medina offspring to know each other well with frequent visits to the island, a pattern already started over the past months as everyone rotated helping the senior Enrique recover.

Little Enrique's arms relaxed as he settled into deeper slumber. Carlos grinned over how well he could already read his son's cues. Lilah had opted to take a year's leave from her hospital duties, but Carlos made a point of coming home for longer lunches to give his wife a chance to nap. He cherished the time with his son. And he looked forward to time with his wife.

Without a doubt, today's afternoon wedding and reception had exhausted the baby for what should be a nice long stretch.

Duarte and Kate had insisted their ceremony include everyone from the most senior member—the king—to the babies. Medina gatherings were a frequent event now, with so much to celebrate in their expanding family. They'd packed even the spacious mansion during the past week before the wedding. Little Enrique's baptism had brought out relatives from Lilah's side as well. And while she still harbored reservations about her father, she was able to enjoy her parents' delight in their new grandchild.

Now the time had come for Carlos to round out the day with a final—private—celebration with his wife. He dropped a careful kiss on his son's forehead then backed away quietly.

Tugging his tuxedo tie with one hand and nabbing the baby monitor with the other, Carlos strode toward the sound of spraying water emanating from the bathroom. He flung his tie aside and plucked a rose from the sterling silver vase beside the bathroom door. He ran the rose under his nose before stepping into the steam-filled room.

He set the nursery monitor on the marble countertop and opened the fogged glass door. "I need to talk to you," he repeated her wording from eight months ago when she'd stunned him, dazzled him with her bravado at confronting him in the men's locker room. "And this is the only place I can be certain of catching you alone on an island full of family and our son asleep in the next room."

Water slicked down his wife's body, caressing every luscious inch as he would soon have the privilege of doing in deliberate, leisurely detail. Motherhood suited her well in every way.

"Well, you most certainly have my attention," she said, gathering her water-darkened hair and stretching her arms overhead with a come-here smile.

He stripped off his tux in record time and stepped under the heated spray, rose in hand, eager to explore the new curves childbirth had brought. "And I'll be doing my level best to keep your attention through the night."

"Am I about to be the lucky recipient of another of your amazing medicinal massages?" She looped her arms around his neck, her slick body against his. Warm pellets of water engulfed them from the multiple showerheads.

"My most thorough massage to date." He plucked the petals free and tossed the stem back onto the bathroom floor. Grabbing a bar of French soap, he lathered his hands into a mixture of suds and petals, then rubbed the fragrant mixture over Lilah's creamy skin. The flowery scent saturated the steam along with the perfume of her shampoo.

"Mmm…" She arched into his touch with a throaty sigh. "We should insure those hands. I am such a very lucky woman to have found you."

"I'm the lucky one, and you can be sure I won't forget that for even a second." He stroked upward until he cupped her face. "I love you, Mrs. Medina."

"And I love you, Dr. Medina."

* * * * *

Silhouette® Desire

COMING NEXT MONTH
Available April 12, 2011

REQUEST YOUR FREE BOOKS!

2 FREE NOVELS PLUS 2 FREE GIFTS!

Silhouette

Desire ®

Passionate, Powerful, Provocative!

SDES11

*Selene wanted nothing to do with the father of her son,
Alex; but Aristedes had other plans...that included them.*

*Read on for an sneak peek from
THE SARANTOS SECRET BABY by Olivia Gates,
available April 2011, only from Harlequin Desire.*

"You were right to turn my marriage offer down," Aristedes said.

And Selene found her voice at last, found the words that would not betray the blow he'd dealt her. "Thanks for letting me know. You didn't have to come all the way here, though. You could have just let it go. I left yesterday with the understanding that this case is closed."

Before the hot needles behind her eyes could dissolve into an unforgivable display of stupidity and weakness, she began to close the door.

The door stopped against an immovable object. His flat palm.

"I can't accept that." His voice was low, leashed.

What did her tormentor mean now? Was he ending one game only to start another?

She raised eyes as bruised as her self-respect to his, found nothing there but solemnity and determination.

Before she could voice her confusion, he elaborated. "I never let anything go unless I'm certain it's unworkable. I realize I made you an unworkable offer, and that's why I'm withdrawing it. I'm here to offer something else. A workability study."

She leaned against the door, thankful for its support and partial shield. "Your son and I are not a business venture you can test for feasibility."

His gaze grew deeper, made her feel as if he was trying to delve into her mind, take control of it. "It's actually the other way around. I'm the one who would be tested."

She shook her head. "Why bother? I know—and *you* know—you're not workable. Not with me."

His spectacular eyebrows lowered over eyes she felt were emitting silver hypnosis. "You're right again. Neither you nor I have any reason to believe that isn't the truth. The only truth. It might be best for both you and Alex to never hear from me again, to forget I exist. But then again, maybe not. I'm only asking for the chance for both of us to find out for certain. You believe I'm unworkable in any personal relationship. I've lived my life based on that belief about myself. I never really had reason to question it. But I have one now. In fact, I have two."

Find out what happens in
THE SARANTOS SECRET BABY by Olivia Gates,
available April 2011, only from Harlequin Desire.

Harlequin Blaze

red-hot reads

Sunny, sensual Hawaiian spring break...again!

Three best girlfriends are recapturing an amazing spring-break
vacation they had a decade ago.

First on the beach is former attorney and all-around good girl
Mia Butterfield. Meeting up with her boyfriend of old is a bust,
so she's shocked when her hero turns out to be someone she'd
never have expected...

Find out who it is in
SECOND TIME LUCKY
by acclaimed author
Debbi Rawlins

Available from Harlequin Blaze® April 2011

Part of the sensual miniseries,
Spring Break

Part 2: Delicious Do-Over (May)

A *Romance* FOR EVERY MOOD™

www.eHarlequin.com

HB79607

PRESENTING...THE SEVENTH ANNUAL
MORE THAN WORDS™ ANTHOLOGY

Five bestselling authors
Five real-life heroines

This year's Harlequin More Than Words award recipients have changed lives, one good deed at a time. To celebrate these real-life heroines, some of Harlequin's most acclaimed authors have honored the winners by writing stories inspired by these dedicated women. Within the pages of *More Than Words Volume 7*, you will find novellas written by Carly Phillips, Donna Hill and Jill Shalvis—and online at www.HarlequinMoreThanWords.com you can also access stories by Pamela Morsi and Meryl Sawyer.

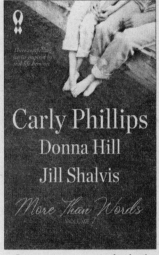

Coming soon in print and online!

Visit
www.HarlequinMoreThanWords.com
to access your FREE ebooks and to nominate a real-life heroine in your community.

Proceeds from the sale of this book will be reinvested in Harlequin's charitable initiatives.

MTWV7763CS

Harlequin® Romance

MARGARET WAY

In the Australian Billionaire's Arms

Handsome billionaire David Wainwright isn't about to let his favorite uncle be taken for all he's worth by mysterious and undeniably attractive florist Sonya Erickson.

But David soon discovers that Sonya's no greedy gold digger. And as sparks sizzle between them, will the rugged Australian embrace the secrets of her past so they can have a chance at a future together?

Don't miss this incredible new tale, available in April 2011 wherever books are sold!

Harlequin®

A *Romance* FOR EVERY MOOD™

www.eHarlequin.com

HR17722